Sweet Berries

C.M. Nascosta

MEDUAS
EDITORIALE

Meduas Editoriale

Contents

CHAPTER ONE

One

She was too horny to think.

Grace was forced to admit that everything currently wrong with her life at that precise moment in time boiled down to that one salient fact. As the lamp above her head swung like a great pendulum, ticking down the seconds until she made a huge fucking mistake, she was forced to confront the ugly truth. She was too horny to think rationally and was about to make a miscalculation in judgment born of imprudent arousal and nothing more — the worst sort to make. As the shadow of the pendant lamp swung over her, the tiny part of her brain not flooded in dopamine and still capable of sense hit the alarm. *It's time to leave!*

They had started the evening off at Gildersnood and Ives, but the trendy gastropub was a mecca for the happy hour crowd, always tightly packed with office dwellers and employees of the various businesses in the commerce parkway, and that night had been no exception. Grace had sighed in relief when it was decided they were wasting their time at Gildersnood, hoping that meant she could go home.

The CSA pickup was her longest night of the week. The program she had started had become so successful and grown so large, that the pickup window had been steadily lengthened to accommodate all of the orders. The day began at her normal crack-of-dawn hour at the farm, but she didn't come home until after dark on pickup night, even in the summer, when the balmy heat of day kept the sky a swirl of violet and pink until well into the evening. There would already be stars winking in an indigo sky by the time she finally pulled her little car into her driveway on pickup nights, and as she'd explained to Caleia earlier, she would be exhausted.

"Okay, but literally I don't understand why. You just tell these folks 'oh good, I'm glad you managed to show up on time, on the agreed upon date, even though it makes no difference to me because you've already paid. Take your shit and go.' See? Easy."

Grace had glared up at Caleia's words, the green-skinned dryad standing over her imperiously before the pickup table, front and center on the farm's wide, circular turnaround. They had still been at the farm when the last customer had finally left, gripping the hand of her rambunctious little boy to prevent him from tearing off again. Grace was certain the little amphibian had licked every single piece of farming equipment kept on the circular drive with his darting blue tongue, so she'd hastily called for one of the farm hands to help carry the woman's bags back to her car, so that she could wrangle her slobbering child.

She didn't bother explaining, knowing her friend wouldn't understand, and perhaps more importantly, Grace didn't want to sound ungrateful. She loved everything about her job on the farm and her life in Cambric Creek; loved her coworkers and friends, and wouldn't trade these long CSA nights in for anything, as they were proof that she was doing good work here. That didn't mean she wanted to social-ize tonight. She didn't know why bars and clubs made her anxious but each and every time felt like the very first day of school — too crowded, too weighted with expectation, and she was horribly out of place. There always seemed to be half a dozen unspoken rules in pubs, rules she was expected to know immediately upon entering, despite the fact that they seemed to be different from establishment to establishment; rules that other people seemed to know instinctively. She'd never been one of the cool kids growing up, and she supposed it was far too late in life to become one now. Besides, she had been *on* for more than twelve hours at that point. Going home was the only thing on her agenda.

"What happened to 'I'm going to start getting out more? I'm going to start being more adventurous?' You act like you're eighty. What do you need to rush home for? To have your bowl of mushed peas and tuck into bed after Wheel of Enticement?"

There was no use arguing with the dryad, a lesson Grace had learned well over the course of their friendship.

"Fine," she'd cried, throwing up her hands in defeat. "I'll go. Happy now? We still need to break down these blackberries before we leave, so don't go disappearing."

Caleia grinned in triumph; a smug, cat-that-got-the-cream expression on her pert face.

"Yeah, actually I am. This is supposed to be your summer of fun, remember? You said you wanted to be more adventurous, and I'm honor-bound as your friend to make sure that happens. Brogan is coming, sooooo, you know. Let's see where the night takes us, shall we?"

She winked pointedly, and Grace felt heat move up the back of her neck at Caleia's words as she mentally recounted the previous afternoon. The big bull had been flirting with her since she'd started at the farm, and as she'd reciprocated the flirtation, things had steadily escalated to whispered comments and innuendo that would be likely grounds for termination at any business with an HR department. Fortunately for her employment, Cal's farm possessed no such thing, but they were beginning to toe a dangerous line.

Cambric Creek was in the grip of a heatwave, and even though she started each day with a light cardigan over her sundress, by early afternoon she would be stripped down to the spaghetti strapped shift, while baking beneath the small umbrella at her table. She had just led a small group of newly arrived patrons up the pathway of the north field, instructing them on where they could start picking their own fruit, before detouring around the back of the first barn, in hopes of finding some shade as she journeyed back to the blistering hot concrete pad where her table resided. Brogan had been coming out of the barn, stopping short as he saw her approaching, a lascivious grin spreading across his bovine mouth as he ogled the amount of bare skin she was showing.

"I'm just about to take a break. How about you? Ready for one?"

She'd smiled, not slowing until she was right before him, feeling the drag of his gaze over her body, biting her lip as he shifted, adjusting the front of his jeans with no trace of subtlety.

"I hadn't planned on it just yet . . ." It would be easy to pretend she were the innocent recipient of unwanted advances, Grace thought as she looked up coquettishly, but it would have been a lie of the most heinous sort. "What did you have in mind?"

He didn't step aside as she moved between him and the barn wall, the press of his huge body even hotter than the blazing sun. Her breath had caught when he'd crowded her against the wooden exterior of the barn, the outline of his cock pressed to her front, a meaty hand dropping to her hip, holding her there.

"Far be it for me to be inappropriate in the workplace, but if you care to join me for an off-the-clock lunchtime rendezvous in the back barn, I can guarantee you won't walk right for a week."

She didn't want to date the big minotaur. She didn't want to get involved with anyone from work. She was smart enough to know that it would only bring trouble. Grace loved her job, loved the people she worked with and the community they served, and she wouldn't do anything to jeopardize that. That did *not* mean, as her hand involuntarily raised to scrape her nails over his denim encased erection, that a very base part of her, the part she was somewhat ashamed to admit existed, wasn't desperate to be fucked stupid by her coworker. *Too horny to think.* Her ex had been a minotaur as well, and while she knew better than to paint the whole species with his tarnished brush, her experience saved her from needing to employ too much imagination to visualize what her coworker was packing below the belt.

She could easily envision exactly how long and thick his cock would be, and knew all too well the delicious pressure that came from being filled by something with that girth. There was a touch of truth to the fantasies she harbored, and as a consequence, she knew how good it would feel to let Brogan lead her off to one of the empty outbuildings, hold her up, and fuck her against the wall. She could almost picture the giant puddle of his release that would be left in the grass, the dirt, or wherever it was they would choose for their illicit assignation, once it had gushed out of her. She would hobble back to her little table on shaky legs with cum-smeared thighs, her cunt gaping open from the shape of him, and ripples of her orgasm still shivering up her spine as she retook her place, smiling brightly to greet community shoppers, schoolchildren, and other daily visitors to the farm. She didn't need to try hard to imagine exactly what she'd be getting by fucking her coworker, and that made resisting his completely inappropriate overtures that much harder.

"Oh, well that seems *very* inappropriate for the workplace," she murmured, pressing herself a little tighter to him, squeezing where she thought his balls would be, her cunt quivering when he grunted in response. "Besides, CSA pickup is tomorrow. Being able to walk properly for that seems sort of important."

"Not inappropriate at all," he disputed in a low, sultry voice. "If I wanted to be inappropriate, I would have told you that the sight of you in that little dress is making my cock hard, and I want to lick those pretty tits while you ride it. See the difference? Completely appropriate."

Her ears had been hot when she finally edged past him, squeezing his hard cock a final time, squinting in the sunlight his big body had buffered.

"When you put it that way, you're right. I suppose you were being completely appropriate. But I really do need to get back to my table."

Brogan had chuckled, shrugging. "Well, I guess that decides my lunch plans." When she'd raised an eyebrow questioningly, he rubbed a hand over the bulge at the front of his snug jeans. "I'm going to head over to the milking place, I guess. I got a list of chores that need to get done today, but I need my balls emptied before I can focus on any of them. Since someone in her little dress went and filled them up."

It wasn't the first time that their flirtation and innuendos had crossed the line to outright sexual propositions, but she knew if she strolled back to her own work and made a point of avoiding him for at least a week, the counter would be reset and they would go back to harmless little quips and comments . . . until things escalated once more, and he was offering to fuck her over the hood of her car at quitting time.

It was a mistake going out that night, a mistake seeing him away from the farm only a day after his lunch time suggestion. Their little game of 'will we or won't we' was fast becoming a game of 'when will we,' and Grace wasn't sure if she wanted to take that step. She knew it wouldn't be smart, and no matter what else she was, she had always tried to be smart. She *wanted* to straddle his wide hips, wanted to get down on hands and knees for him, wanted to let his over-sized cock graze her tonsils as he fucked her into the next fiscal quarter. She wasn't stupid enough however, despite Caleia's inference, to actually allow it to happen, no matter what she wanted, or how embarrassingly easy it would be.

Their party had pressed through the crowd to the bar upon arrival at Gildersnood that evening, had waited what felt like one hundred years before the beleaguered bartender finally made their way down to their end of the polished wood. By the end of the first round, it had been obvious that no tables in Gildersnood would be turning over for them anytime soon. When Zeke, the livestock manager, cheerfully announced they'd simply have to relocate to the Man-o-War, Grace had been the only one to groan. She knew she could have left. She was a whole-ass adult woman, and no one could tell her what to do, but she also knew Caleia would bitch at her if she left. To the Man-of-War she'd dutifully trudged, and unsurprisingly, Brogan had managed to take the seat beside her.

"I'm going to hit the head, no one had better finish my drink while I'm gone," he'd cheerfully announced to the table, pushing back his chair. As he stood, he leaned down, horns cutting through the air until his lips grazed the shell of her ear. "I'm pretty sure this place has a backdoor down by the restrooms," he breathed into her hair. "It would be a wild coincidence if we both found ourselves in that hallway in a few minutes. The back lot has gotta be nice and secluded this time of night."

The light above the table swung haphazardly as the big minotaur straightened up, bumping the pendant with an errant horn. Laughter from her inebriated co-workers echoed around the table, but Grace quickly glanced down, cheeks heating, not wanting to see the loaded smile on his face. *Too horny to think.* Accepting his invitation would be a bad idea. She knew that, knew it in spite of the way her pussy throbbed at the thought. She'd already been treated to the wide spread of his warm palm on her leg beneath the table, his thick fingers teasing at her inner thigh until weakness and horniness had made her capitulate, opening her legs and granting him access to the space between.

"How ticklish are you, Grace?" he'd asked innocently, a murmur for her ears only. She hadn't needed to answer, her resolve tested a moment later when the tip of one of his thick fingers began to dance over the front of her panties, seeking her clit and finding it with ease, chuckling when she jumped. "There she is." Back and forth, back and forth, the tip of his finger stroked, teasing her until the thin material was drenched from her arousal. He'd been playing that game for the last half hour, and she could only imagine how hard his cock had grown as he'd tickled her clit.

She knew it would be a bad idea to accept his proposal, but it would be just as poor of a plan if she stayed. If she were still here when he returned to the table, she already knew she would let him slip a meaty digit beneath the edge of her panties to see just how wet he'd made her, let that finger sink home, a preview of what his cock would do, and that would be that. She'd let him fuck her that night, as many times as he wanted, until his balls were drained and they were both satisfied, and Bad Decision Boulevard would welcome its newest resident to the Dumb Bitch Court condominiums.

"I need to go," she exclaimed, the moment Brogan had disappeared, pushing back from the table. "I-um . . . it was a really long day, and I'm exhausted. Thanks for the round, Zeke. I'll see everyone tomorrow!" Caleia was on the other end of the table, and Grace didn't give her the chance to challenge her words. She needed to hurry up and get out of that bar before Brogan came back and she slid beneath the table to suck his cock right there in front of their coworkers. She left to the sound of everyone's cheerful goodbyes, breathing in a lungful of the humid night air the instant the

Man-o-War's door had swung shut behind her. Keeping the top down on her little farm-branded convertible car, she hoped the rush of cool air would bring down her heated state on the drive home.

The pungently sweet smell of blackberries enveloped her as she zipped up the quiet streets, like a secondary advertisement for the farm, as if the branding on her car wasn't enough. The flat of blackberries on her backseat was part of an order for a troll family who'd been in the process of moving the last time she'd spoken to them, and hadn't been at that evening's pick-up. When she'd reached out to Cal earlier to make him aware, he'd insisted on the blackberries being divided amongst the employees, pointing out that they'd been picked two days prior and had been sitting in the hot sun all afternoon. Everything else could be requisitioned back to the farmstand shop, but the blackberries would be too far gone. She'd made a note in her phone to reach out to the family in the morning to cancel their account before next week, before helping Caleia section out the berries, taking home a double share when one of the farmhands who'd been on-hand to load cars insisted they would go to waste in her house.

Grace tried mightily to distract herself as soon as she got home. Dropping her bag on the kitchen counter as she entered the side door, she decided to throw herself into busy work — emptying the dishwasher, rinsing the berries, carefully laying them on a cookie sheet to flash freeze — but the attempted distractions did little to dispel the arousal itching beneath her skin, or the way she pressed her thighs together as she separated the cutlery — igniting the tingle the minotaur's teasing touch had sparked. *Too horny to think.* It was no use. She was simply prolonging the inevitable, she thought with a sigh, turning off the lights and locking the side door. She needed to be fucked, and since she was smart enough to not allow her coworker to do it, she needed to take care of business herself.

Caleia was right. She needed to get out more. She needed to get out and meet someone, even if she wasn't sure if she was ready for a relationship yet. Otherwise, she was likely to become horny enough to go writhing around on the sidewalk like a cat in heat, yowling and offering her pussy to any passersby that wanted to fill it. The thought of one of her neighbors — maybe the satyr across the street, middle-aged with a bit of a paunch, or perhaps the house of university students, young men of varying species housed on the corner — coming across her like one of those ridiculous, needy cat girls, and pulling out their cocks then helping themselves, made her dizzy with desire. *You're so far gone, you'd let them all take a turn,* she thought with a little moan. That tiny part of her brain that had made her leave the bar had since been flooded with the rest of her body's arousal, and the thought of allowing the satyr across the street to rut her in the middle of her front lawn as a line formed behind him was extremely enticing. Grace knew if she didn't go upstairs right then and there, she might go across the street and knock on the man's front door. The swing on her screened-in porch seemed as good a place as any for the tray of berries. They would keep until morning, but the persistent ache between her thighs would not.

The day had been humid and the evening just as warm, but the light breeze coming in through the open bedroom window was cool, and it was a relief to pull the sundress she'd had on since early that morning over her head. As she turned to toss the sweat-dampened dress into the hamper, a muffled *whump* sounded in the tree just outside the window, rattling the branches. Whirling in surprise at the noise, Grace waited for a limb to go crashing to the ground, or for the screech of an owl, but several moments passed and nothing stirred. *Too horny to think, now you're hearing things.*

The soft breeze whispered over her breasts as the lace-edged bra joined the dress in the hamper before she tugged the soaked panties down her hips and kicked them in after. She was able to smell her own arousal, still wet from Brogan's teasing. Co-workers, she reminded herself, were tricky things. She'd made the right choice, the *smart* choice, and when push came to shove, she could take care of business on her own. The finger she pressed into her folds came away slick, and as she dragged the moisture across her clit, Grace couldn't help sighing in pleasure.

An answering whicker came from outside the window, freezing her with her hand still between her thighs. There was something out there.

Instantly her skin prickled at the sensation of eyes resting heavily upon her.

Something . . . some*one?*! — was there, in the tree, watching her from the darkness. The thought alone of some unknown being just outside her window should have been unsettling. The reality that someone was watching as she undressed *should* have been terrifying, should have made her lunge for a towel or her robe, to *hide*! Instead, her nipples tightened at the thought, helped along by the slight breeze, and a fresh ripple of desire heated her core. *You **did** say you were going to start being more adventurous* . . . The wet heat of her sex seemed to pulse in agreement against her fingers still pressed there, eliciting another soft moan from her throat. Sure enough, the branches outside rustled in response, as if her voyeur was trying to get a better look.

Grace felt a flush spread across her body — up her neck to the tips of her ears, down her throat and across her chest. She was fair skinned and blushed easily. Whenever she was nervous or anxious or embarrassed she would flush the color of a tomato. It had been especially bad when she was still in the bridal game, for it seemed every deep-voiced, commanding-voiced father-of-the-bride or demanding groom who cornered her to question an expense sent her pulse hammering in her throat and a burning flush spread up her neck. She knew without question that her cheeks were probably rosy pink right now, matching the redness across her breasts, but arousal was racing neck and neck with nerves, with desire outrunning good sense. *If they want to watch, you ought to give them a good show . . .*

The view from the bed was centered in the middle of the window, and her mystery watcher had a clear view as she lowered herself to the mattress, slid to the middle of the quilt and opened her legs wide. This wasn't how she'd envisioned the evening ending when she'd left the bar — she'd anticipated some quality time with her vibrator and thoughts of her minotaur co-worker spurring her on. Instead, the sound of soft clicks and chirps seemed to surround her, making her oh-so-aware of her audience, leaving the vibrator forgotten in her nightstand, at least for the moment.

It could have been *anyone* out there, she considered as her head tipped back, exposing the white of her throat to her unseen voyeur, pinching her already hardened nipples. After all, Cambric Creek was an interspecies community and prided itself on its diversity. She kept a hand at her breast, kneading and squeezing, while the other traveled down her body, skating across the soft swell of her stomach and over round hips. Grace was fairly certain she was one of only a few dozen humans living here, and the unknown factor of her audience was thrilling. *Maybe it's someone cute*, she considered as her fingers sought to soothe her aching clit. She moaned at the first touch, pleasure rippling up her back, louder and more wantonly than she may have done without an audience. Her fingers circled the sensitive bud, trapping it and squeezing until she cried out again, settling into a rhythm that left her hips rocking. Steady circles, medium pressure, and thoughts of her watcher. It was bliss.

Despite the little gasps of pleasure coming from her mouth, she held her breath every few moments, pausing her movements to listen. There was a steady hum coming from outside like a low-frequency vibration, raising the hairs on her neck, and when she pressed a finger into herself, pumping it slowly, the vibration increased. Every time she stopped moving, a distressed chirrup sounded from the tree, as if her audience despaired of the show ending prematurely. When she again resumed rubbing circles against her clit, whoever it was would give a click of satisfaction, earning another moan from her in response. The extra set of eyes had her racing towards a climax, far faster than it normally took, the knowledge that someone was watching more exciting than she could have ever imagined. *This was a much better choice than staying at the bar.*

Thinking of her watcher, she added a second finger, wondering what sort of anatomy her audience possessed, rubbing into the spot that made her toes curl. She wondered if her voyeur was pleasuring themselves at the sight of her; what sort of cock they possessed or if they possessed a cock at all. Grace tried to imagine who it might be, *what* they might be — a lizard person, perhaps, with an affinity for climbing trees? Two cocks, red and straining, maybe with frilled edges and spikes. She wondered how they would pleasure themselves, if it were, in fact, a sleek-scaled lizard man. A hand on each cock, stroking them in an alternating rhythm? Holding them together, to pump in unison? Her hips were lifting off the bed now, as her fingers thrust in and out, desperately wanting to be filled. She wondered if the lizard man would crawl right through her bedroom window, stuffing her full of one of those bright, red cocks; wondered if they would both ejaculate at the same time, or if he came once from one and then a second time from the other. It would be messy, her rational brain protested, but just then she didn't quite care about being rational, and the thought of two erupting cocks was *delicious*.

Or perhaps a batperson, like the one who'd been in line ahead of her at the Food Gryphon the previous week, who'd been loudly complaining to his companion that his balls were being compressed by the skinny jeans he wore. She tried to envision that same batperson now, tight jeans open and his fat testicals swinging free in the night air, as he jerked off to the sight of her touching herself. *Would they be hanging upside down? Wouldn't that make a huge mess when he cums?* She'd never had a partner of either species, and the un-known element made her thoughts race, but she was certain that whoever was out there—watching as she masturbated for them — was pleasuring themselves at the sight.

Her head felt heavy, and she was desperate to reach her peak at that point, her breath hitching. Her fingers were no longer good enough, and Grace knew even if she were to add a third, it would still not be the tight squeeze she desired. When she ceased her movements, withdrawing her hand, the unseen presence in the tree clicked its disappointment again. She rolled, stretching until she could reach into her bedside table. One of the finest perks of being an adult living alone was the freedom to purchase any sex toy she desired, she thought. Literally every species under the sun had a corresponding dildo available online, with varying degrees of extra bells and whistles.

It had been Brogan's cock she had been fantasizing about over the past several weeks, fat and heavily veined, with a toe-curling mid-shaft swell to stuff her full, but she was impatient, and she knew from experience that taking a minotaur cock required some working up to, even one made of silicone. So it was a goblin model she reached for then, not big enough to require any stretching, but with enough girth to give her something to clench around as she came. A quick slick of lube from her nightstand, and then she was swiftly rolling back to the center of the bed, hoping her audience hadn't abandoned the show.

She moaned again at the first press of the bulbous head against the lips of her sex, sinking it in until the fat goblin head popped into place. Grace pumped it shallowly, never pulling the tip out, all too aware of the buzzing frenzy from the tree outside, as if her voyeur found the sight of her fucking herself even more exciting than watching her rub her clit. She began to do both, putting each hand to work, her toes curling against her light summer quilt, knowing she wouldn't last long at this point. She was too tightly wound, too desperate, too horny to think.

Beyond her window, the buzzing hum had reached a fever pitch. She wondered how close they were, if they were ready to explode; wondered if it would spray out in a gust like a selkie, if they would shoot thick, splattering ropes of pearly-white release like an orc, or if their knuckles would be coated as it spilled down their shaft.

A series of staccato clicks joined the humming from the tree, and she wondered if that was the sound of her audience reaching their peak and orgasming just beyond the light of her room. The thought of their messy release was enough to push her over the edge with a gasp. Her heels dug into the bed as she arched, crying out and clenching around the goblin cock. Blinding white pleasure that wiped her vision overtook her, leaving her legs shaking as it throbbed through her, her clit pulsing against her fingers until she sagged to the mattress, completely spent. She whimpered, pulling the dildo out. She hoped her voyeur could see the glistening string of slick, drooling from her body, still connected to the silicone head as she pulled the goblin model free, evidence of how much she'd enjoyed the performance she'd given them.

A heaviness descended on her then, pushing her eyes shut almost without her consent. She vaguely remembered crawling beneath the thin summer quilt on the bed, her head finding the pillow without needing her eyes. Soft, comforting chirps issued from the tree as she settled, the low, purring hum providing a cocoon of sound, lulling her into a deep, satisfied sleep.

Two

"I still don't understand why you left! He's cute, right?"

Grace huffed out a breath, forcing a bright smile as a tractor wagon of wildly waving children rumbled past. It was camp week, the first of several the farm would host, and greeting the children, processing them in, and explaining the rules of the farm ate up a small chunk of her morning, as it would for the rest of the week. She turned to the dryad once the tractor had pulled the kids out of sight and rolled her eyes dramatically.

Caleia was the farm's recordkeeper, the tree to which she was tied being the largest and oldest on the property. There was no Farmer's Almanac or field manual that could predict seasonal rainfall with the pinpoint accuracy that she could, nor was there any computer system in existence that shared her long memory for soil rotations, late frosts, and annual yields from each and every tree. She didn't concern herself with the animals, but when it came to the trees and crops, Caleia was the farm's most valuable resource. The nymph had been the one to show Grace around on her first day and had quickly become one of her closest friends, but she was also, Grace thought with a scowl, a first-rate instigator.

"So what if he's cute? What does that even mean? Lots of people are cute. Who cares?! He's cute, but he's also slept with half the town. *And* I don't need to be screwing around with someone I see every day," she plowed on, ignoring the tree nymph's attempt to interrupt. "That will just make work awkward and I like it here too much to screw things up. There are a million guys in the world, I don't need to fuck around with one I'm forced to see every day. So stop trying to make this happen, because you're not going to win."

"Ugh, *fine*! You know, you make it really hard to have fun when you're so damned responsible all the time."

The memory of the free show she'd given to the mystery watcher in her tree the night before heated her cheeks. *Not always so responsible.* She'd woken that morning with a slight headache, somewhat surprised to find herself naked beneath the quilt, until the slick slide of her thighs brought the previous night's activities roaring back. She laid in bed pinching the bridge of her nose well past the time she normally got up, contemplating all that had happened the evening before. She'd nearly had sex with her coworker. She'd masturbated in front of an unknown stranger, possibly a creeper, potentially one of her neighbors. *Impulsive, irresponsible, incautious. You're lucky you weren't murdered.*

She'd still been sex-slick as she attempted to shower away the heaviness in her head, reaching a hand out to steady herself against the wet shower tiles as her fingers stroked into her heat, coating themselves in the viscous evidence of her continued arousal. She'd come against the pulsing pressure of her showerhead wand before dressing for the day, trying to put the previous evening behind her. The sight of her neighbor had her face flaming scarlet as she got into her car that morning, returning the balding satyr's wave, remembering *those* thoughts with a groan. *You're practically ready to turn this into a spectator sport. 'Come fuck the horny human on Persimmon Street, bring a friend!' Maybe Caleia's right. Maybe you really should just let Brogan fuck you, get this out of your system once and for all.*

"You certainly cut out early last night," he'd breezed casually that morning, approaching her table with his normal self-assured swagger. While the outline of his huge horns cut an impressive shadow across the pavement, her cheeks had still been warm from the previous night's audience, the slick between her thighs caused by the remembrance of a buzzing hum and odd little chirps. The pendulum of her game with her minotaur coworker had once again swung into the 'won't we' direction, and she had her voyeur to thank for it.

"I really wasn't in the mood for much socializing," she'd answered as sunnily as she could. "Like I told Caleia, I really don't like going out on pickup nights." It was innocent and innocuous, but he got the message, leaving her with a small chuckle. She knew his feelings weren't hurt, and it was just as likely that he hadn't gone home alone that night. Brogan's reputation preceded him — he was a well-known fuck boy, but he was still a good guy. *That doesn't mean you need to screw things up at work by sleeping with him.*

Cal cantered up the long drive as she shook the thought away. "How big was that troll family?! We restocked enough food to fill the cases again. I'm not gonna lie and say I'm not happy to sell it twice, but can we make sure we get a hold of them?"

"Already did it. Talked to the wife this morning, asked if she wanted anything shipped, and she said no. Didn't even want a refund, so I guess we can think of it as their donation back to the program. I'm pretty sure they had like eight kids, so that's actually a pretty big order off the books, I'll probably need to book two families into their slot to match the spend."

The big centaur spat in the dirt with a chuckle. His sharp eyes and brusque demeanor had intimidated her when she'd come for her interview, but since that first day, Grace had been delighted to learn that Cal was eager to embrace her ideas on bringing the farm into the current century.

"It's a digital age," he had moaned that day, shaking her hand and welcoming her to the team. "I guess it's about time we at least had a CrowdJournal page."

He enjoyed reminding everyone who would listen that he was a fifth generation centaur farmer, that this land had been in his family's possession long before Cambric Creek was incorporated as a town, and rather than roll her eyes the way the rest of the staff did whenever the oft-repeated tale was trotted out, she had endeavored to make it a part of the farm's branding.

Saddlethorne was a Cambric Creek landmark, she wrote in their new ad copy — ads themselves that were brand-new, her first budgetary expense — just as historic as the Applethorpe Gardens; just as important to the community as the waterfall's overlook bridge, commissioned a century earlier by Erastus Slade; and far older than the crystal chandelier hanging in the domed foyer of the old public theater building on the center of Main Street where Jack Hemming kept his office, on the center of Main Street. "For five generations, Saddlethorne had been feeding the community," she wrote, "a leader in Cambric Creek's booming agricultural segment, and a hub of activity for visitors, young and old alike."

"Who did this?" he had demanded after the first half-page spread had run in the community's small local paper. She'd not been sure how to answer, meekly raising a shaking hand that day, as Caleia and Zeke exchanged confused looks. Her face had been like a tomato as he read the ad aloud, certain she was going to need to find a new job already, when Cal folded the paper down, revealing a sharp-edged grin. "You wrote that bit about Jack's office?" She nodded again, but Cal had already thrown his head back in laughter. "And they said I didn't need to hire someone," he rasped, dropping the paper on her table. "Been here two weeks, and she's already worth every gods-damned penny." When the piece of newspaper turned up in a small picture frame hung on the office wall, Grace realized she was safe.

She wasn't certain if Cal had initially thought she would do anything for his business beyond creating a few social media pages and booking the farm for a handful of weddings each year, but he knew better now, frequently joking that if he were to start an employee of the month program, her face would grace the walls over and over again.

"Well, I have no doubt you'll have those slots filled by the end of the day. Looks like another full schedule for the week."

"Two more camp groups are coming in today, and the Woodlands Scouts want to get something on the calendar. We have six weddings this month, so maintenance really is going to have their work cut out for them."

Cal laughed again. "If maintenance is looking thin, Zeke is going to learn to push a broom. Keep up the good work, ladies!"

They watched the big centaur canter off, heading in the direction of the barns, and Caleia rolled her eyes.

"You really are the biggest kiss ass. Don't think you're off the hook. Just because you know how to book weddings doesn't mean I'm going to let you throw yourself into farm events every single day for the whole summer. You're going to meet someone if I have to drag you out by the hair every night of the week."

Caleia's words had more than an edge of truth, she knew, but that didn't stop her from preening under the taciturn centaur's frequent praise. *If only Torm could see you now.*

After all, event planning was a dead end career, as her ex had so frequently chided her.

She had been finishing a hotel management and hospitality degree when they'd met, and had fallen into the wedding planning business completely by accident. Tormand was in construction, working his way steadily up the ladder at the company he'd been with since he was practically a teenager, from the grueling labor of the job site to the more comfortable confines of the site office. She was working as the assistant venue manager at a hotel, helping wedding planners every week. Torm worked long days and she was gone nearly every weekend, and it hadn't been long before the cracks had begun to show. One contact had led to another, and before she'd known it, Grace was spending all of her time planning happily-ever-afters for other people, as her own relationship deteriorated.

"You need to find a real job," he would grumble in the evenings, as she sat before her color-coded spreadsheets, with the neat little boxes she used to compartmentalize every facet of her job, wishing there was a spreadsheet large enough to fit her relationship into as well.

"This *is* my job," she would remind him tonelessly. "This is what my degree is in, remember?"

"The fact that they even offer a degree in party planning is a joke."

"Well, I guess that makes me a clown. But the last time I checked, this joke is paying half our bills." They had been together five years at that point; five years of what she was able to recognize now as emotional abuse — of complaints and gaslighting and tiny insults, like microscopic shards of glass beneath her skin, chafing until she bled, an interior wound that never healed, scraping her raw.

Work had been her escape. She'd thrown herself into her job, finding a headset that fit over her puffy blonde curls without pulling at her ears, a peach-colored leather cover for her tablet which was always in hand as she went over spreadsheets and checklists, and a cheerful shade of cherry lipstick that was neither too garish nor too vampish. She bought a wardrobe of brightly-colored dresses that flattered her pear-shaped figure and heels that were comfortable to run in. She kept an unflappable, sunny smile and a can-do attitude in the face of endless bridal emergencies and rampaging mothers-in-law, rearranged banquet tables herself, and had become fairly proficient at redoing floral arrangements. She arranged veils and straightened torques, moved gumpaste flowers to camouflage slightly smushed cakes, and never went anywhere without a pocket-sized package of tissues to dab at eyes and preserve flawless makeup.

She would stand at the back of the venue, mouthing along as she watched as the happy couple exchanged their vows, did their hand fasting, lit their candles, or broke their glass. *I Tormand, take you Grace, into my heart and my home, to be my mate.* She was able to still perfectly envision the way he'd looked, looming over her that day in the courthouse, repeating the lines the magistrate fed; was nearly able to smell the overpowering lilies she'd carried that day — an arrangement of stargazers — but she could not remember herself speaking back the vow.

She remembered the way they'd argued that morning, frustration with the car, a mishap with her bouquet, and the hastily purchased lilies. All signs of things to come, she should have known. The flowers represented wealth and ambition but said nothing of love or devotion, and she'd taken care to ensure the brides under her watchful eye had not made the same mistake with their own bouquets. She ensured that *their* big days went off without a hitch, a promissory note for their futures, and she did so with a smile. It didn't matter to anyone that inside she felt as if she were screaming. Screaming in a locked, windowless room where no one could hear her, and even if they could, no one cared.

Work was her solace, and so she made work the focus of her escape plan. Finding a job had been the first step to emancipation. Find a job and secure housing, that's what she had read on the websites she scrolled through on the laptop at work — instructions on how to leave, what to do if there were children involved, shared pets, joint bank accounts. She was luckier than most, Grace assumed. They had no kids, no pets, and a single joint account. The only thing with which she'd be leaving was the mental exhaustion of half a decade of emotional bullying, and she was certain that was enough. She made dreams come true every week for strangers, put everyone's feelings before her own in her private life, and she was at the end of her tether. Running away seemed childish and cowardly, but she couldn't come up with a better plan, and the more she thought about freedom from her current predicament, the more running away had appealed to her.

She didn't want to run far. Her plan's only requirement had been to put Bridgeton between the place she was leaving and wherever it was she was running. The big city seemed like an impenetrable moat between the life she was leaving behind and whatever the future held. She still wanted to be within a day's drive of her family in case there was an emergency, to be able to see old friends if the occasion ever arose and didn't wish to completely cut herself off from every contact she'd made over the years.

Working for a farm would never have been something that occurred to her. The job listing was technically for a social media director, which was not her specialty, but the whole thing had been clumsily worded, with only the vague shape of a recognizable position hidden within a quagmire of con- tradictory priorities. It was as if the person doing the hiring wasn't quite sure what they were even looking for, so she took a chance and responded and Cal all but confirmed her suspicions the day she'd interviewed..

She'd expected to be disappointed. Tormand had taught her that disappointment and recrimination lurked around every corner, and she expected them now, but when she'd arrived at Saddlethorne that first day, driving up the long, narrow dirt road, passing fields dotted with sheep and sway- ing crops, all she saw was possibility. Ahead loomed a large red barn, like something from a painting, and beyond it,

Grace could see rolling green fields, dotted with picturesque outbuildings. She knew at first sight it was perfect. The big centaur knew, at least in theory, that they ought to have some sort of social media presence, to help people find them when searching for pick-your-own fruit farms, something more than the cursory profile pages Caleia had created and then promptly abandoned several years earlier. When she asked him if they ever hosted weddings on site, he told her about the grand weddings hosted by a winery up the road, wistfully adding that he wished they had the capacity to do something like that, seemingly oblivious to the fact that the farm already possessed everything it needed to become a community hub.

She liked to think that it was serendipitous, the fact that she had found the posting at all, and that she in turn was the one who had responded. She brought her years of experience and contacts and the gut-deep certainty that she could turn Cal's operation into something magnificent, and Saddlethorne provided her with the safe haven she desperately needed: a fresh start, a distraction from her dumpster fire personal life, and a project to lose herself in.

It had been nearly three years, but the thought of putting her heart back on the line made her stomach tighten and her head swim.

"There's just so much going on right now. I'll start dating when things aren't so busy," she promised.

Caleia just rolled her eyes. "You mean when the pumpkin patch opens and we're doing apple picking and hayrides every day? The busiest time of year? Oh, okay, sure."

The rest of the week passed in the same busy blur as the week prior, a flurry of activities to direct and schedules to manage. The days skipped by, and before Grace knew it, her little foray into exhibitionism was nearly a week-old memory.

The details of that night had danced on the tip of her tongue as she sat across the table from several of her friends during the weekly tradition they tried hard to keep, meeting at one of the swishiest bistros Cambric Creek had to offer. The conversation over dinner had turned, as it almost always did, to their respective love lives. Ennika, giggling over her wine glass, encouraged Grace to download Growlr, a popular multi-species dating app, and she had laughingly protested that she wasn't in the market for werewolves.

"It's not just werewolves!" the goblin insisted. "Don't pay attention to the name. It's for every species!"

"Are you going to pretend you'd kick a single one of the Hemmings out of bed for shedding in the sheets? I think not," Caleia snorted, leaving the whole table wheezing in laughter. "I think they should bring back those charity calendars firemen used to do. Pose nude with nothing but your big firehose for a good cause, Trapp. Think of the children."

Grace dropped her head in her arm as the tiefling couple at the table beside them turned to glare in their direction as they all shrieked in laughter. The Hemmings were, without a doubt, the most attractive residents of Cambric Creek — a clutch of dark-haired werewolf brothers with sparkling eyes and wide, white smiles. Every woman who worked at Saddlethorne managed to find a reason to crowd into the office twice a year when the most handsome member of the town's fire department accompanied the fire marshall as he completed his inspection. It was a wonder they weren't setting fires on purpose just to bring him out more often.

Ennika and Caleia had insisted Grace download the dating app right then and there, screeching in protest when she attempted to use her work headshot as her photograph, insisting she use a cropped-out photo of herself wearing a low-cut dress sparkling with sequins from a wedding reception they'd all attended at the farm several months earlier. For the rest of the hour their table had cackled with laughter as they swiped through match after match, squealing when they recognized someone.

"This is the manticore from the bank! I *knew* he looked kinky. Anyone that meticulous over the bills facing the same way is going to be into spanking, that's an obvious tell."

"What about a naga, Grace? I'm pretty sure I recognize him, he lives over by Sandmar. He says he works from home and his hobbies are gaming and foreign films."

"That's probably code for he watches a lot of catgirl porn," Caleia cut in. "I say pass." By then, one of the nearby tieflings was grumbling over their laughter, and was being shushed by his companion.

"Seriously though, we have to find you someone this summer."

"You're wasting your breath," Caleia interjected, earning Ennika's scowl as she downed the rest of her bright blue drink. "Mushed peas and an early bedtime is all this one is interested in."

"I never said that!" Grace grumbled. "You're trying to get me to hook up with our coworker. I'm sorry if I have better judgment than you, that doesn't mean I'm eighty."

Across the table, Tula frowned. "You shouldn't bury a bone in your own garden, everyone knows that."

"*Thank* you." Grace stuck her tongue out at Caleia, as a dignified response. "And aside from the fact that he's my coworker, that I have to see him every day, and that he is probably the last person in town I should even consider sleeping with, my ex was a minotaur! I understand, they're two completely different people, but this is a multi-species town. Frankly, I think I could afford to branch out a bit."

Tula raised her glass in a one-sided toast, and Caleia threw up her hands in defeat. "Fine, whatever. I give up! Enjoy your mushed peas and Wheel of Enticement. I'll bet Mr. Catgirl porn aficionado has some really cool body pillows you could borrow to help with lumbar support for your early bedtime."

The temperature outside had not dropped, and as she left the air-conditioned confines of the restaurant, Grace swayed in the humid night air, the conversation still ringing in her ears. She knew her friends were only trying to help; knew they didn't really understand her reticence over dating again, and how could they? She'd not disclosed the details of her failed marriage to any of them, hadn't talked about Torm or the way he treated her to a single person.

It was probably a mistake, she knew. She needed to find someone to talk to, needed to find a therapist to work through any lingering unconscious issues she harbored from the years of cutting remarks and gaslighting. She needed to find a way to get over this hump of not wanting to trust anyone with her heart again . . . but knowing and doing were two different things. Besides, as she told Caleia, she *was* very busy. *It's going to take someone really special, and really special doesn't just drop out of the sky.*

She was certain she wasn't ready to risk her heart. She wasn't sure if she was ready to use the app for dating . . . . but she just might use it for some meaningless hookups. The itch Brogan's flirtations had ignited beneath her skin had not abated; if anything, her exhibitionist evening had only fanned the flames. She didn't need to see a therapist to know that her actions were utterly preposterous — if she wasn't willing to risk her heart by dating again, why *was* she willing to risk her safety, masturbating for some unknown presence outside her window? She'd woken two nights earlier, certain she'd heard the sound of something heavy landing in the tree, but no further sound came. She'd had an early morning and rolled over to go back to sleep, and the thought that her voyeur had returned hadn't occurred to her until the following afternoon.

She thought about her mystery audience again as she trudged up the stairs of her little rental house, after she arrived home. She wondered if they were on the app, if they had potentially been one of the faces her friends had scrolled past that evening, wondered if they truly *were* one of her neighbors. She pondered, as she pulled her dress up her body, if they had, in fact, returned to watch at her window, disappointed at the lack of a show. She'd only had two drinks that evening with dinner, two fruity little things that had barely made her tipsy, but she would still blame them in the morning, she thought while kicking off her panties and unhooking her bra. Kneeling in the center of her bed, knees spread shoulder-width, she cupped her breasts and arched her back. It was a balmy, humid night, but there was a bit of a breeze coming in her window, just as it had been that night earlier in the week. Her nipples hardened as she teased them, puckering into tight, rosy buds that she pinched be-tween her thumb and forefinger, rolling until they twinged, a pull she felt behind her navel. Grace dropped her head back, letting her curls graze her back, as she bounced the heft of each breast in her palms.

She nearly missed the muffled *whump* in the tree outside her window, and might have been able to convince herself she had only wished she'd heard it, but as she stretched a hand down her body, a familiar chirrup sounded. They *had* come back, had possibly been coming back for days, she realized with a start. She wasn't as clouded by mindless lust as she had been the night she'd come home from the bar, and the rational part of her brain was quick to remind her that this was a bad idea. It was one thing to have done this once, but to escalate the behavior . . .

She wouldn't do it again, she told herself. Tomorrow she would fill out a proper profile on the Growler app, would start getting out and meeting people, would find a real life partner with whom she could work out a bit of her sexual frustration. Tomorrow, she would start using the app tomorrow. Tonight, Grace thought, biting her lip, she would scratch this itch one more time. The unknown presence beyond her window hummed in approval as her fingers slid between her legs, stroking into her heat. She was wet already, dropping her head back again with a sigh as she rolled over her sensitive clit.

"Do you like watching me?" she murmured, heat moving up her neck. She wasn't sure what she would've done, had they responded with words, but she decided the two clicks she received in return were a response in the affirmative. Her clit felt like a live wire, sparks flaring behind her eyes as she rolled over it, already swollen and sensitive, as it had been for the majority of the past week. *Too horny to think.* She wondered what it would be like to offer herself up to the presence outside her window, letting them reach a hand in to stroke her. *A hand or tongue,* she thought with a little moan. "It's too bad you're not a little closer," she spoke into the empty air. "If you were, you might be able to take a taste."

That was what she needed, she considered, not a date. She could buy her own dinner, and making mindless small talk with a stranger wasn't going to cool this fire in her blood. She needed someone to go down on her until she came against their tongue, and then fuck her until she was boneless and finally able to get a good night's rest. She'd not been sleeping well, between the heat and her horniness, and there was no doubt in her mind that all she needed was a good licking and a deep fucking, and she'd be able to get her head back to normal. Lowering herself to her back, she slowly opened her legs.

Her bedroom window was on the side of her house, and while the distance between her house and the neighbor's was not terribly far, there were several large trees, like this one. Come wintertime, she'd be able to look out her bedroom window with an unobstructed view, directly to her neighbor's house. Now though, the trees were heavy with their greenery, blocking any line of sight her neighbor may have had to peer into her house. She had checked after the last time, rushing to the window once she got home from work the following afternoon, the thought having occurred to her on her drive home. She'd sagged against the sash in relief, barely even able to see the neighbor's house at all, and as she opened her legs for her audience now, she was comfortable in the knowledge that no one might be spying from next door.

No one was peeping, she thought as she dragged her fingers through her slickness, except for her Peeping Tom. Another huff and click from her voyeur, a bit closer sounding, she thought, as if they had moved into a better position on the branch's front row. The thought made her stretch her legs open even further. *We want them to have the best view, after all.* This was stupid and risky, and Grace knew she would hate herself in the morning, but at that moment, she couldn't bring herself to care. She moaned as she rubbed her clit, circling it with several fingers.

"Too bad you can't take a taste," she repeated, knowing she was both tempting fate and playing a dangerous game, but the promise of a satisfying release was her only focus. She imagined the same lizard man from her previous fantasy, climbing through her window and licking her clit with a flickering blue tongue, his two red cocks bobbing as he focused on her pleasure. Or perhaps, she moaned again, the bat person. His tight jeans would be open, cock standing at attention as his fat testicles bounced in the open air, climbing over the jamb, wings opening wide as he feasted on her cunt, nibbling her clit with gentle fangs.

Grace realized it was the one element that had been missing from her flirtations and innuendos with Brogan at work. The big minotaur was always quick with a quip about his size and how small she was in comparison; bringing attention to the not-at-all subtle bulge at the front of his snug jeans. Even his propositions had been rather singularly focused — he offered to fuck her, promised she wouldn't walk right for a week, and had insinuated that what she needed to solve whatever problem she'd been grousing over was the thickness of his cock between her legs. Never once had he made any allusion to going down on her. *Selfish*, she thought with a huff. *They have big dicks, and they think that's all they need.* Her voyeur would be focused on her pleasure, she was certain. After all, they had been happy just *watching* her pleasure. *Reason number 942 why it was a good idea to not go home with Brogan*, she thought, sinking two fingers into her heat.

She wasn't sure how long she had been fingering herself for her unseen audience, only that the buzzing and chirping clicks seemed so close and so loud in her ears, it was as if they were practically in the room. Much like the last time, her fingers would not be enough to put her over the edge, but she had no shortage of aids to get her there. Sliding off the bed, she retrieved an innocuous looking bolster pillow from behind her bed pillows, and the goblin dildo and lube from her bedside table, pushing the bed a foot closer to the open window. *If you're going to give them a show, you may as well let them see everything.* The pillow had been purchased from the same online store that sold the multi-species models, and had been worth every penny.

Straddling the pillow, she coated the bulbous silicone head in a generous dollop of the lube, whimpering as she rubbed it against her labia. She teased the tip of the head at the mouth of her sex, letting just the tip push in before raising herself, spurred on by the buzzing coming from the tree. When she sunk down onto the squat length with a gasp, it clicked in approval, several chirps of appreciation accompanying the dildo's wet squelch as she began to rock.

It was too bad she was swearing off all of this after tonight, Grace thought as she fucked herself on the goblin cock. Again, the presence of her audience left her barreling towards release, far faster than her solo play ever yielded before. A pity this would be the last time, she considered, thinking she might have begun with a little striptease next time, if she were going to repeat the performance.. She could start slowly, getting herself in the mood, teasing her pussy to wetness instead of diving right in, already dripping in arousal. She was too far gone tonight to make it last, and she knew as soon as she started rubbing herself, she would be done for. Her thighs tightened around the pillow as she increased the speed of her rocking, raising her hands to cup her breasts once more.

That was when it happened.

Something flicked over her clit, something that was not her fingers. Nothing had appeared in her window yet there was no tree-climbing werewolf suddenly in her bedroom, no random Hemming appearing with tongue extended, nor was her imagined lizard man or bat person there framed in the moonlight. Her goblin dildo had not suddenly sprouted an extra appendage, but then it happened again — a flicker over the sensitive pearl of her sex, then another, and another. Grace moaned as the flickering little licks continued, her hips nearly losing their rhythm.

Her peripheral vision caught a flash of movement, and she realized she could have simply put her hand down and caught whatever it was if it continued, but where would that have left her? She had no doubt that whatever it was, was coming from the buzzing presence outside her window, and if she stopped it, she was only hurting herself. *Too bad you're not going to do this again.* The flicking lashes came more often then, almost as if whoever was in the tree grew bolder when she did not stop them. Her breath began hitching, her moan coming out as a wheeze. It felt *incredible* and she wanted to finish this way, common sense be damned, so there was no incentive to stop them.

Her high-pitched gasps seemed sufficient to telegraph her intention of allowing them to continue, a chirrup of approval coming from her voyeur, right before the lashing little licks abruptly stopped. Her eyes popped open. Her head was swimming, and she was nearly dizzy from how close she'd been to her peak, aggravated that they'd stopped. *Maybe they're gone. Maybe someone saw them. Maybe they're at the front door, breaking in at this very moment-* The pressure returned, a caressing flick before it fastened over her swollen clit, sucking with the steady, unabating pressure of a vacuum, and the world went white. Lightning shot up her spine, making her go rigid, as if she really *were* a live wire being sucked to electrocution.

She'd never had an orgasm quite like this, one that twisted behind her stomach, making her legs shake and go numb; her whole body trembling, every nerve ending she possessed coalescing into one. It all centered on her clit, which was still being sucked by her thirsty voyeur as if she were the last glass of water on earth. All she could do was grip the edge of the pillow she straddled and hold on for dear life as she shook.

Grace felt her vision begin to go spotty. She had never come this hard, nor for this long, the pleasure beginning to border on pain when the suction released. Whatever it was had wrapped around the swollen, throbbing bud, enveloping it in a slippery embrace, tugging gently as she slumped. Her muscles had clenched so tightly around the goblin dildo, she nearly felt cramped. She might have been embarrassed by the squelching pull of the slick-coated silicone any other time, but it was all she could do to keep from toppling over at that point, and she realized she was far past the point of mortification.

It was a shame she would be giving this up, Grace thought again, as a cloud of heaviness descended upon her once more. If she came this hard every night, she might never have issues sleeping again. She didn't bother covering herself as she dropped back against the mattress, eyes closing. Her mystery voyeur was still delivering gentle little licks to the side of her sensitive but satisfied clit, with a contented click and a chirp being the last thing she heard before she slipped beneath the veil of consciousness, and the world fell away.

CHAPTER THREE

Three

"I would love the opportunity! Yes, we can definitely accommodate the carnival rides. Our south lot is completely paved over, it's normally used to house farm vehicles, but those can all be taken off-site for the duration of the event." Grace scowled, waving off two of the farmworkers whose conversation around the coffee cart had spilled into her workspace. "Yes, with a south entrance . . . yes! Perfect, that sounds good to me! I look forward to meeting you then!" She huffed in annoyance once she ended the phone call, glaring at the backs of the retreating farmhands.

She'd started the harvest festival the year she began working at Saddlethorne, inviting the community crafters and merchants who populated the weekly Saturday Maker's Mart to set up booths of their wares on the blacktopped surface of the southernmost lot, hiring a few small food vendors, and that first year had been a great success. The pumpkin patch had been nearly cleaned out, cornstalks and bales of hay were loaded into the trunks of cars and the back of pickup trucks all weekend, fodder for Samhain decorations all around town. The vendors had seemed happy with the turnout, and Grace had invited them all to return again the following year. Since then, the annual fall festival had gotten bigger and bigger, to the point that local merchants and vendors now vied to rent space on every available foot to peddle their wares to the throngs of people who showed up for the haunted corn maze, hayrides, ziplines, and other activities she'd dreamed up. The town's planning committee had evidently taken notice.

"We have a meeting on the books," she crowed into her walkie talkie, then grinned hugely at the excited whoop from the goblin who ran the market stand. Cal and Caleia instantly began to speak over each other, but a school bus had just pulled in view, coming up the long dirt road, carrying the campers she was prepared to receive.

Grace was glad to have something on which to focus. It had been nearly a week since the night she met her friends for dinner, nearly a week since she'd once again given an X-rated performance for the unseen presence beyond her window. Almost a full week of quiet evenings and empty nights. Despite being certain her voyeur had been coming back previously, they had stayed away since that evening. Even though it was ridiculous and she had vowed to give up the potentially dangerous habit, she couldn't help the way her stomach twisted, as if she had done something wrong.

She'd awoke sometime in the middle of the night, after that last performance, finding herself still laying atop her quilt, legs still slightly spread. Her head had been heavy as she'd slipped beneath her sheet, listening to the thump of the forgotten dildo hitting the floor, then quickly falling back to sleep. For the next two nights, she paid attention to the sounds outside of her house, listening keenly for any hints that *they* had come back. She had resolved to stay downstairs and keep her clothes on, but there had been no sounds, no hint of anyone or anything in the tree. By the third night, she'd felt befuddled by their continued absence, and by the fourth, a bit put out. It had been risky behavior on her part and she was well rid of the temptation, but that didn't stop her from feeling as though she'd been dumped. *Dumb bitch court it is.*

Having something to throw herself into at work was a welcome distraction. After all, she reminded herself, the community planning committee was, in the microcosm of this town, a big fucking deal. Being the venue of choice for the official community celebration would be a tremendous coup; planning the celebration would be both time-consuming and all encompassing, and Grace felt like she could use the distraction.

The rest of the afternoon passed in a blur as she did intake for another group of campers, then dealt with a stream of phone calls. The sky was just starting to turn a dusky violet, long fingers of pink stretching to the horizon where the sun puddled to crimson when she began to end her day by powering down the computer and closing up the small office trailer. The outside table would be open for another hour, giving the community's nocturnal customers a chance to make CSA arrangements. She'd just pulled out a chair at the outside table, pausing to gaze at the bucolic sight of the farm at dusk when a long shadow loomed behind her.

"E-excuse me . . . " The voice was low and deep and sent an undulating shiver up her spine before she turned to survey its owner.

It was a mothman, tall and reedy, with long, leanly muscled arms and legs, a solid-looking chest, and a concave stomach. Grace stared transfixed, watching as his long jaw worked, and she was certain if his throat hadn't been concealed by a thick mantle of fluff that trailed down his neck, she'd be able to see the hard swallow he gave. It was then that she realized she was staring openly. *Way to go, real smooth.*

"Hi!" she squeaked, attempting to make up for her rude-ness with enthusiasm. "How are you this evening? Are you looking to set up a CSA subscription?"

His long, fluffy antennae fluttered a bit before he began to speak.

"Hi . . . um, I-I wanted to—"

The sound of branches snapping under the feet of a worker who was returning from the fields made the low hum of the stranger's voice break off as his head whipped in the direction of the noise, and she used his momentary distrac-tion to take another look. His wings had raised slightly at the sounds, large and delicate-looking things with a rippled pattern, dotted with large eyes near each wingtip, the same unusual color as the velvet that lightly coated his skin. He seemed to possess a slight iridescence, and she wondered if his color changed with the light. Currently, he was the same shade as the rapidly darkening sky—smokey violet deepening to grey. Grace didn't pretend to be a Cambric Creek expert, and she certainly didn't know everyone in town, but she had never seen this mothman, and she knew without question she would have remembered him.

For starters, he was unclothed, although that wasn't necessarily uncommon. Clothes were a tricky thing in an interspecies community, she had come to learn. The act of wearing clothing was looked at by many as an exclusive affectation of prudish humans and highfalutin elves, while the act of walking around with one's balls swinging in public was viewed as barbaric by others. Cambric Creek's current mayor, she was told, had been elected largely on a "freedom of dress" platform, although the basic community guideline seemed to be if one's genitals were carried on the outside of one's body, then one should respect thy neighbor and cover said genitalia. She could clearly see he fell into the *innie* category of resident; his abdomen an unbroken line of smooth gray velvet, protruding hip bones, and surprisingly solidly muscled thighs. Whatever genitalia he possessed, it was kept on the inside, meaning clothing was not strictly required. Most of her coworkers and friends fell into the *outie* category, and seeing someone completely bare was somewhat jarring to Grace, even if it was technically allowed. *Probably not for much longer. I hope he owns pants.* The election wasn't until the fall, but it was expected that a new mayor would be soon taking office, signaling an end of pantslessness in Cambric Creek.

She raised a hand in parting to the passing farmhand before turning back to the tall, nervous-seeming moth. Grace remembered how hard it had been being new here — the tight-knit community was extremely friendly, but it was, in fact, tight-knit. She had been lucky, luckier than most humans in town, it seemed. The town she'd grown up in hadn't been mixed species the way Cambric Creek was, but it was not entirely human, and she had gone to school with goblins and trolls, and ogres, had mingled with them at University, and in general, knew how to get along with her mixed species neighbors. From the outside though, she knew from experience that Cambric Creek could seem daunting to a newcomer. This tall stranger had an air of timid skittishness about him that she found sweet, and Grace decided she could be the person who welcomed him into the fold. When his garnet eyes found her once more, she gave him a gentle smile.

"Now," she murmured softly, "what was it you needed tonight?"

His mouth opened and closed several times, with no sound coming out. Her question seemed to have stymied him. She had begun to wonder how long she would be sitting there in the growing darkness as he gaped at her like a choking bullfrog, when he seemed to land on a word.

"B-blackberries."

The deep vibration of his voice made something twist in her stomach and the hairs rise on her neck. The farm had a pick-your-own blackberry field, it was true, but she knew for a fact that the ripest berries had been picked out for the CSA drop, just as they had the week prior. Grace had the strange certainty that blackberries were not what he had come seeking. He'd been casting around, and had grabbed onto the fruit, for whatever reason. She wasn't sure *what* the true answer was, but blackberries, she'd wager, were not actually it. She wasn't sure if he suffered from social anxiety or was perhaps just a cute weirdo, and she had no idea what odd association his mind had made as he mouthed silently at her, but unfortunately, he had chosen the one thing she was certain she couldn't actually provide.

"Do you like blueberries? I know the late blueberries looked really good this morning."

His eyes widened slightly, his mouth opening and closing again as if he had never heard of a blueberry, as if the very concept of produce in general was foreign to him, and she gave a little sigh of exasperation.

"I-I suppose?" he hummed hesitantly. *Berry? What's a berry? What is fruit? Why are we here?* "No . . . blackberries?"

He couldn't stop fidgeting, shuffling his feet in the gravel and wringing the long, spindly fingers that dangled from his hands. *Definitely a weirdo.* She gave him another smile, not wanting to disappoint him on his first visit to the farm when he was obviously shy.

"Well, we can go check the field, but it might be a few days until they're really sweet. We had the majority of this early crop go out in orders this week . . . "

She'd bent to retrieve a flashlight from the box under the table as she spoke, and he issued a disappointed chirp at her words. A chirp she recognized immediately. Grace let out a startled yelp, banging her head on the underside of the table, pain reverberating across her skull. She saw stars as she staggered backward, spinning unsteadily to see the mothman, grabbing the side of the table to keep from falling. Her flashlight had rolled several feet away, its beam illuminating the grass at their feet in a way that made her feel as if she were in a horror movie. One she'd seen before. *The one about the dumb bitch who masturbated for a freaky stranger, who stalks her and finds her at her job just before he puts her in his trunk.*

"It's *you*!"

The tall moth recoiled slightly at her words, his antennae flattening against his head, wings raising. It was hardly the picture of intimidation, and she straightened up in response to his panic. *Oh, no you don't.* Garnet eyes darted around, and she quickly stepped forward before he could make good the escape he was obviously contemplating.

"You — *you* were the one outside my window! But . . . why did you come here tonight? Wait, how did you find me?!" *Why didn't you come back?* The question was there, hovering on the tip of her tongue, but she couldn't bring herself to admit how much she'd enjoyed her short-lived career as an amateur exhibitionist, and how put out she'd been when he'd not returned. Gazing up, Grace took in his sharp cheekbones and panicked expression, suddenly remembering that flickering pressure against her most sensitive parts — the most satisfying orgasm she'd ever enjoyed, and the most erotic experience she'd ever had in her life. It was hard to believe that *this* had been her unseen partner in that act, and the very thought made her whimper in mortification. *You practically fell over that night and he saw the whole thing.*

The slender moth still looked as though he were contemplating escape, his eyes casting about, his wings fluttering nervously. He had an appealing silhouette: lithe and lean, impossibly tall . . . the exact opposite of her stocky, barrel-chested bull of an ex. *Well, you wondered if they were cute, now you have your answer.* Those incredibly long fingers wrapped around his muscled forearms as he fidgeted, clicking in distress.

"How did you find me?" she repeated, holding her arms out slightly, as if she might be able to block his escape. He suddenly seemed to have a hard time meeting her eye, and she had the distinct impression that if he'd been able to blush, he'd be scarlet.

"Y-your car." The deep hum of his voice was little more than a whisper now, although the low vibration of it still made her shiver. Her boxy little convertible was wrapped with the farm's logo, it was true, and he'd had a clear view of it in her driveway from his position in the tree that night. "I'm *sorry*," he blurted out suddenly, urgent chirps accompanying his words. *It's kind of adorable*, she thought of the small sounds he made. "I-I didn't *mean* to watch you. I mean, I did, but I didn't mean to. I shouldn't have. I should have left. I smelled . . . I smelled the berries. I love blackberries, and it's been so long since I've had them. Do you have any idea how hard it is to get farm fresh fruit in the city? I stopped in your yard when I smelled them, and then I-I . . . got distracted."

His wings fluttered nervously, the fluffy antennae atop his head twitching wildly.

"By me?" she blurted. "You got distracted by me?"

He nodded miserably and she was absolutely certain he'd be blushing if he could. The thick fluff around his neck and shoulders looked incredibly soft, and her own fingers twitched, wanting to reach out and touch the velvet of his chest. She burned in mortification at the thought of him stopping in her yard, lured in by the delectable scent of the ripe berries in her screened in porch, like an olfactory spot-light — only to see her undressing before her open window.

"I smelled the f-fruit . . . and then I smelled you."

Grace jolted, pulled from her reverie by his words, her jaw dropping open. "You smelled *me*?!"

"You smelled amazing, much sweeter than the berries. I-I wasn't able to help myself." The notion that he had been able to smell her arousal made her clap a hand over her mouth. She wondered if her other neighbors who may have possessed a heightened sense of smell were able to tell when people were walking around with damp panties. "I'm so sorry. I wanted to apologize, I flew past your house the one night to see if you were home to leave an apology note, but then I thought maybe you had an alarm or cameras and I didn't want you to wake up, and-and then—"

"And then you watched me again," she finished for him, feeling fire spread up to her ears.

You smelled sweeter than the berries. The next time he'd stopped outside her window, she'd invited him to take a taste. And he had. He was nearly vibrating with remorse as he nodded, those long digits knitted in a gesture of supplication, and she gave him what she hoped was an absolving smile as she flushed at his words.

"I'm so, *so* sorry. I feel like I violated you and that's not what I intended. I-I just wanted to let you know."

"Well . . ." she sucked in a breath, squaring her shoulders, "you don't need to be. Sorry, I mean. Please . . . I'm not mad. I-I had fun that night. Both nights. We're both consenting adults, aren't we? If you didn't want to watch, you could have flown away, and I could have closed my damned curtains. And I'm very glad to meet you, now at least I know it wasn't some creep."

His fluffy mantle puffed up at her words, feathery antennae lifting, and the noise he made was very nearly a purr. *Okay, it's not kind of adorable, it's completely adorable.* "Okay, let's go out to the field. I'm not making any promises, but like I said, the next crop will be ready in a few days. Now you, um . . . have a reason to come back. Right?"

His name was Merrick, and by the end of the hour, she was smitten.

"So, you said you lived in the city? In Bridgeton?"

He'd only recently moved to Cambric Creek, he'd haltingly confessed as she led him through the darkening fields. Grace wasn't accustomed to traversing the farm this late in the evening, and certainly not alone, but most of the staff was long gone, having started their workdays before dawn. It was only her little table and the farmstand shop that stayed open to accommodate later visitors. Although, she considered, as they moved past the picked out rows that had been the burgeoning strawberry fields just a month earlier, adding a special night of the week to the pick-your-own fields for nocturnal residents was an excellent idea. She beamed up at her skittish companion, thrilled with the idea, one that wouldn't have occurred to her were it not for his late-evening visit.

"N-no, I've been living up north, right on the unification border."

She glanced up in surprise. It was cold and snowy for much of the year near the border, and he didn't seem robust enough to live under those conditions. *Especially walking around with no clothes on.* "I didn't think moths liked the cold," she said with a smile, biting her lip when he shuffled nervously.

"Oh, I-I don't. If I hadn't been there for work . . . believe me. Last place I want to live."

"And what is that you do?" She was looking up, so she saw the moments when his dark red eyes darted down to meet hers hesitantly, fully prepared to remind him that not only did he know where she worked and where she lived, he had sought her out.

"I was working at a university, I'm a-a research scientist. It was in the middle of the city," he added. "All the fruit in the grocery store was trucked in, hothouse produce." He huffed in slight disgust, and Grace grinned widely. *Okay, so he's heard of a blueberry before.*

"How interesting! What is it that you research?" They'd nearly reached the field at that point, and she realized she'd taken him on a bit of a detour around the fallow strawberry patch. *Hopefully he didn't notice.*

Another askance look, hesitating a long moment before he continued. "I study the agricultural impacts on the migratory habits of seasonal pollinators." Another swift glance down. "You know, like bees and hummingbirds?"

"Yep, I know what a pollinator is." He had the good grace to look abashed for a moment, the feathery antennae on his head flattening down around his temples. "What do you mean by 'the agricultural impacts?' Do you mean farms or city planning? You know, the garden club here, they plant all the flowers in the park and up the medium on Main Street, and they make a point of doing a pollinator garden. Do you mean impacts like that?"

"Every individual action is helpful, of course," he said seriously, his voice taking on a slightly surer tone as he continued. "But expecting individual yards to solve the pollinator problem is like expecting individual citizens to single-handedly end plastic pollution by switching to reusable straws.

Individual citizens can't reverse the impact of climate change, and a patch of wildflowers up the median strip isn't going to account for the damage done by monoculture farming. Not that it's a bad thing," he added hastily, as if he'd realized how dismissive he sounded, his antennae bobbing once more. "It's great that they're doing that, and I saw that the local schools have a field garden that the kids maintain, and that's great. But obviously habitat loss plays a huge part, of course. Suburban sprawl necessitates construction in woodland—"

"Yeah, but this is an unusual area," Grace cut in. "I've lived in the suburbs my entire life, and I've never been this close to actual farms before. And the city is literally just a half-hour away! I think they do a really great job preserving the green-space around here."

"This area is unique," he agreed slowly, with the air of someone choosing their words carefully. "I've not seen an agricultural sector this large so close to the urban metropol-itan area, at least, not very often. It's actually why I'm here, to study the effects local agriculture plays on the pollinator population in the surrounding areas."

He continued to talk, his voice having completely lost its nervous stammer. He was passionate about what he did, Grace could tell, his deep voice ringing with the surety of someone who was clearly booksmart, all of his shyness and nervous tics forgotten for the moment. *He's cute. A little awk-ward. Definitely a cute weirdo. Kind of a dork, but that's cute too.*

"So how long have you been here?"

He ducked his head nervously again once the conversation moved away from his work. "Um, about t-two weeks? I'm renting a place in a development called Applebrook? The family who lived there moved away just a few days before I moved in. I'm renting an apartment they had, not the main house."

"Oh, I know that area. It backs right up to the Applethorpe wood, that's really nice. Wait, are you renting from trolls? I know that family, they were customers of my CSA program here." Grace realized he had likely moved in only a few days prior to watching her from the tree the first time. *What a welcome to the neighborhood.* "Well, here we are. Like I said, it's pretty picked out, you're not going to find too much ripe fruit in here until the middle of next week, probably."

As they wandered together through the berry patch, she thought he seemed more at ease beside her. He told her a bit about his work studying the migratory patterns of butterflies and bees, making her laugh with stories about the baby bats he'd nursed who thought he was their mother. She told him about the farm, her job there, and how much she'd loved living in Cambric Creek so far. It was the nicest evening she could remember spending with someone of the opposite sex in ages.

"You're going to love it here, everyone is really welcoming and friendly," she smiled up at him in the darkness, seeking his red eyes and blushing to find them already trained on her intently.

The words had barely left her mouth when she stumbled on an unseen rock in the field. His arm shot out, catching her shoulders and preventing her from falling, and she clung to his forearm as she regained her footing. She had a feeling that her labored panting had nothing to do with her near fall. The forearm she gripped was like a steel cord, flocked in smooth, grey velvet. Heat curled through her, remembering the last time he'd perched in the tree beyond her window.

Grace recalled exactly how she performed for him, how she touched herself, the way she'd straddled the pillow holding her toy, and that she'd opened her legs wide for him. She remembered that teasing flickering against her clit, and the technique with which he had sucked on it with whatever mystery appendage he possessed. She swayed again, her unsteadiness having nothing to do with the rock in the field. She held fast to his strong arm long after she'd steadied her-self, wanting to nuzzle his velvety skin. He was so incredibly tall that she barely came up to the middle of his chest, putting her at a perfect height to press her nose to his soft sternum. She wanted to run her hands down the long length of his body, wanted to discover what secrets it held, finally letting go of him with a blush when she realized they'd come to a standstill. *Get a grip!*

He'd only managed to collect a small amount of the sweet fruit, clicking and vibrating in disappointment, the familiar sounds bringing another flush to her face when something inside her snapped. *I'm supposed to be getting out, being more adventurous. Putting myself back out there. He's brand-new to the area, doesn't know anyone . . . who better to show him around?* She wanted to find out exactly what he'd done to her that night and what he'd used to suck her until her brain practically melted and ran out of her nose. *And I want him to do it again.* She wasn't interested in putting her heart on the line, but she would be *very* interested in getting to know this shy mothman a bit better. She didn't want to sleep with her coworker, didn't especially want to spend an endless amount of time on dead end dates from the multi-species app, not when she was really only interested in getting laid. It was kismet that he had found her, and Grace wasn't about to look this particular gift centaur in the mouth.

I"know where you can get a whole flat of berries," she offered with a deep breath. "They're super sweet too. I know, I had some for breakfast today. They were flash-frozen, but they still taste like they were picked yesterday."

He chirped at her words, an adorable little vocalization that came from his throat, somewhere behind that enormous mound of fluff. Whether it was from nerves or excitement she wasn't sure.

"I-I don't want to impose on you any more-more than I already have . . . "

Her cheeks burned. He'd hardly been an imposition, and she was eager to find out if the smooth expanse of velvet skin would remain as flush and unbroken if she were able to see it the next time she spread her legs open for his audience.

"It's no imposition," she said quickly. "There's no way I can eat them all by myself, and I hate to see any of them go to waste." He could come back to her place, she thought giddily, stomach swooping in excitement at the thought. She would take him somewhere first, welcoming him to Cambric Creek, something historic . . . "Have you seen the observatory yet?"

"I've passed it, " he answered hesitantly, chirping again. "My office is at the research lab on campus. It-it belongs to the University now?"

"It's maintained by the University and used as a classroom, but it's open to the public. Do you want to meet there? Say . . . tomorrow night? Then you can come back to my place." She was half inclined to invite him home with her right then and there, putting an end to the mystery not only of his velvety physique but how he'd made her come so hard she nearly blacked out. The words were on the tip of her tongue, but there was something in his reticence that made her swallow them down, something . . . oddly adorable? about the way his antenna had flattened around his head, flush against his pointed ears.

"I — wait, I-I can't. I have . . . I have things to do at home."

The excuse must have sounded as shitty to him as it did to her, for the instant the words were out, hanging between them like a particularly fetid dumpster, he clicked in distress, his antennae practically brushing his neck. *A dumpster of **lies***. Heat suffused her face in great red splotches she could feel without needing a mirror to see them. *He's a peeping tom and you're an exhibitionist, of course he's not interested in coming over, what's wrong with you?*

"You-you can come back to my place though?" He'd knitted his long fingers together, twisting his bony wrists and pulling nervously, like an intricate game of cat's cradle without the string. "It's a part of my lab rotation," he went on hastily, "data that needs to be recorded at specific times. I keep everything at home though, so if . . . if you wanted to, we could, I mean you could . . ."

He stopped again, sucking in a deep breath. A shudder moved through him, and he trembled like a leaf, clinging to the end of a barren branch. Grace felt her stomach flip-flop again, a low swoop, and she found herself inexplicably holding her breath for his next words. Her own embarrassment seemed a distant place in the face of his near tangible anxiety, eyes closed, and she was certain she would be able to see his Adam's apple bobbing in a hard swallow if his neck were not concealed behind that thick, appealing-looking mantle. She wondered, if she were to bury her face against it, if it would be as soft as it looked; wondered what he smelled like, if his velvety skin carried the scruffy warm smell of a small animal, or if he smelled like the open air, through which she assumed he flew. *Wait, who cares? You want to fuck him, not cuddle with him, remember?* His bony shoulders raised in a resolute sigh before pushing back firmly, and his eyes popped open, trapping her in their garnet gaze.

"I-I came to say I was sorry. I didn't mean to watch you, and I shouldn't have come back, that was appallingly bad manners." Her lips quirked up in a small smile. Ascribing what they had done together as a simple case of bad manners, like the little clicks and chirps he made, was sort of adorable. *Definitely a cute weirdo.* "I know you said you're not mad, but I just want you to know — I *am* sorry. But-but I'd like to see you again, get to know each other, if-if you wanted to. We can meet at the observatory and then . . . then you can come with me, maybe? If you'd like? It won't take me long to record the data, and I have a telescope and there's an excellent view of the Northern Cross asterism from the deck. Scorpius tends to be a bit low and the light pollution from town makes it a bit harder to appreciate until much, much later, but if-if stargazing is what you're interested in, we can still do that. Stargazing and berries?"

Grace stared, somewhat incredulously, shaking herself after a moment. *He thinks you're interested in stargazing.* She suddenly found it very hard to form words, hard to take a breath, hard to think of a good reason why she shouldn't go to the observatory with this tall, attractive stranger. He seemed sweet and shy, if not a tiny bit oblivious, and it was hard to reconcile the actions he'd taken from outside of her window, but Grace had a feeling most of her friends and coworkers would say the same thing about her. She was upbeat and organized and cheerful, and probably the last person they could imagine putting on a pornographic show for a stranger.

"Stargazing and berries," she repeated, smiling up at his uncertain nod. *He's a cute weirdo for sure . . . but why not.* His shoulders were sharp when she gripped them for leverage, pulling herself up to brush his mouth lightly with her own. It was forward of her, and her cheeks burned as she dropped down from her toes, trying not to notice the adorable way his fluffy mantle puffed up, and antennae bobbed above his head. They had gotten the trivial ice breaking out of the way already, hadn't they? They'd already been far more intimate than this, even if they were strangers then. "I can't wait."

She left him in the darkness, raising the spindly digits on his hand in a hesitant wave as she pulled away. At the first stoplight on the way home, she pulled out her cell phone, thumbing it open to Caleia's text thread.

"You're going to be so proud of me."

Chapter Four

Four

Stars already winked in the sky when Grace stepped out of her car at the observatory.

The area around the University was vibrant and bustling, full of affordable counter service cafés and brightly-colored pizza joints, booksellers that bought and sold used textbooks, and more than a dozen other small businesses that catered to half-broke college students.

When she'd started at Saddlethorne, she'd been living in a little apartment on the edge of Bridgeton and commuted each day, reminding herself the forty-minute drive in rush hour traffic was better than the life she'd left behind. The property market in Cambric Creek was fierce and bidding wars over houses were commonplace, the asking prices for said houses well above market value to start with. Purchasing a house in town was a pipe dream, but once the spring semester ended and students began to clear out of their rented homes to leave for the summer, she'd scanned the local real estate listings hourly. When the little yellow house with the gingerbread trim on Persimmon Street became available, Grace wasted no time. She didn't mind the proximity to the university, appreciated the slightly less expensive dining options that existed on this side of town, and the drive from her house to the observatory that night took only a few minutes.

There was only one other vehicle in the parking lot when she stepped from her small car, peering around the dark space. It wasn't altogether uncommon — the observatory was one of the busiest places in town on nights of celestial importance, each month during the full moon, and whenever there was a particularly interesting star or asteroid to be spotted — but on a night like this, a weeknight with no significance on the calendar coupled with the uncomfortably humid weather, she supposed she shouldn't have been surprised. *What's wrong with you? You're supposed to pick public, well-lit up places for dates like this. It's like you went out of your way to pick the darkest abandoned lot in town!*

"H-hello?" She called out weakly, taking a few steps from her car. The gravel crunching under her feet was the only sound. Raising her eyes to the street light above, she gasped at the sight of darting shapes streaking in and out of the beam of white light, swooping and falling. *Get a fucking grip, pull yourself together!* They were little brown bats, the same type that she watched from the deck off her kitchen on summer evenings, nothing to be alarmed over. *This is why people make bad decisions in horror movies. You get jumpy over every little thing. Then some little bats are innocently just flying around and you're too busy focusing on them to notice you're about to be stuffed in a fucking trunk.*

Merrick chose that moment to melt from the darkness at the side of the building just at the edge of her peripheral vision, and she shrieked in surprise. As she spun to face him, her legs became trapped in the unyielding prison of her skirt, her movement faster than the material could keep up with. Grace stumbled, throwing her arms out to steady herself, and it was a full moment before the dress slackened, swinging freely once more. Her fists clenched, as she remembered Caleia's aggravating flurry of text messages that evening.

Be sure not to wear one of your Little House on the Prairie dresses.

That's the opposite of sexy.

And cute underwear!

*You **do** own cute underwear, right?*

The problem with that advice was that she *liked* her boho country dresses, and had never been one for dressing particularly sexy. The revealing outfit Caleia had advised was still hanging on the back of her bedroom door, and she knew the dryad would likely not approve of the long maxi dress she'd worn instead, tiered in lace and dotted with delph-blue flowers, but Grace didn't quite care. The dress was spaghetti-strapped, with a deep-v neckline that hugged her breasts, revealing juuuust enough. She *had* worn cute underwear, the cutest she had, and she was fully prepared for it to make an appearance. If Brogan got hot in the middle of the day seeing her in one of the floral print dresses, Grace rationalized, she decided that was good enough for her date as well. And besides — the shy mothman had already seen what was under her dress.

The shadow he cut across the paved end of the parking lot was huge and menacing. His large wings rose and rustled, antennae atop his head resembling demon horns on his shadow twin. A familiar nervous chirp and click dispelled her momentary panic as she slumped in relief, realizing it was him, noting that he was just as long and leanly-muscled and attractive as he'd been the previous night, as he stood before her small table at the farm.

"Sorry," he called out, wings rustling again. "I-I didn't mean to startle you." He towered over her, and even though his height gave the impression of lankiness, Grace noticed for the first time how broad his shoulders actually were, the width of his back, tapering to an impossibly slender waist. He seemed sleeker that evening, his velvet skin possessing an almost satin shine beneath the overhead light and his fluffy mantle even more voluminous than the night prior. She was struck by the curiously adorable image of him primping in preparation for this date, and gripped the skirt of her dress to restrain herself from reaching out to stroke his arm. *I wonder if he brushes himself.*

"You-you look beautiful." Her cheeks warmed again at his slightly awe-struck words, as if she were some great beauty, and not the reckless human he'd watched masturbating, acting as if she were in heat. His antennae twitched wildly as his arm extended slowly. She wasn't sure if she'd ever met someone so earnestly sweet and anxious, returning his tremulous smile with a brighter one of her own, before she realized he held something.

"These are for you."

The small hand-tie of flowers would have been called a tussie mussie in another age, but they were thoroughly un-expected that evening. Something swooped low in her belly as her fingers brushed his, her nose catching the sweet, heady floral fragrance of the small bouquet. Lily of the Valley. It was late in the season for the pungent, diminutive blos-soms, and she had no doubt the bouquet had been procured at the little shop in town, owned by three identical beetle-like sisters, each with gleaming black hair and iridescent green carapaces. The shop was well-known for being able to pro-cure blooms long out of season, and for its array of exotically cultivated plants.

"I hope you're not allergic. They smelled so nice, I couldn't resist."

She had never had a very good ear for languages. It was a relief that most species spoke the common, even if each had their own language and dialects. She was able to read a bit of Orcish and a smidgen of troll, but the second someone actually started speaking, it was as if something in her brain turned off. Her ears were not able to process the sounds quickly enough to turn them into something recognizable for her brain to interpret, and so she would be left smiling dumbly in the face of the speaker, silently hoping they spoke the common as well.

The language of flowers was different. Much like the common tongue, language of flowers was understood across species. She always knew what sort of arrangement to send in sympathy or in celebration, had silently analyzed wedding flowers for years, making predictions about the happy couple purely based on the flowers they had chosen to celebrate their nuptials. The weight of those showy, overly-perfumed lilies — devoid of love or commitment — were still heavy in her hands, years later. By contrast, Grace didn't need to consult one of her books to know that Lily of the Valley was a symbol of purity and youth across half a dozen different cultures and species, but that wasn't all. *A return to happiness*. She swallowed heavily, lifting the small bouquet to her nose and inhaling, nearly rocking off her feet. *A renewal of love.* She didn't especially believe in fate, nor in love at first sight, and she certainly wasn't looking for love, hoping it would have the good sense to keep its eyes averted if it passed her, but the notion of this tall, velvet-skinned stranger bringing about *a return to happiness* was a bit too on the nose for her liking.

Still, they were lovely, and it was a distressingly sweet gesture.

"I love them," she grinned up honestly, slipping her arm through his, the cord-like steel strength beneath her palm kicking up her heartbeat a few notches once more. His mantle puffed up, his antennae standing straight up on end, possibly the most endearing thing she'd ever seen. It was as if he were *trying* to wear down her resolve, to fall for his adorableness, she thought as he held the door open, ushering her into the observatory's main chamber. *Down girl. You're not looking for a relationship, remember?* Grace squared her shoulders, not loosening her grip on his arm. She wasn't looking for love *or* heartbreak, and their tentative relationship had already been defined by the two nights she'd spent framed in the light of her window. *You're not looking for a relationship . . . but that doesn't mean you can't have fun.*

The circular interior of the observatory was dimly lit and cold, despite the heat outside. The second level was ringed in a wrought iron railing, the only modern thing about the space being the high tech telescope in the center. The other car in the parking lot belonged to an older reptilian couple, both turning to glance over their shoulders with identical sour looks when the inner door was pulled open. The couple had been meticulously recording the positions of stars in a notebook since she and Merrick had entered the space, giving no sign that they were planning on relinquishing their control on the telescope anytime soon, glaring every time their conversation rose above a whisper.

Grace sucked in a lungful of the cool air as they made another circuit around the interior, patiently waiting for their turn. Goosebumps rose on her upper arms as she stepped around a cluster of unused stanchions for the fourth time, and a shiver moved up her back, her nipples tightening ever-so-slightly beneath the thin material of her dress. It was the temperature of the room, she reminded herself again; a reminder she'd issued all four times they'd circled the space. It was absolutely without a doubt the drastic temperature difference in the room, as it had been the second and third times they'd made this short pilgrimage. It clearly had *nothing* to do with the press of his long-fingered hand at the small of her back, gently guiding her around the obstacle, even if she felt the heat of his touch like a brand through her dress, searing her skin.

He's probably not even aware he's touching you. He's just trying to keep you moving, because it will be embarrassing if you stumble, and you've nearly knocked yourself out in his presence once already. The thought tasted like a lie, she was forced to admit. The unwavering strength of his arm, the gentle pressure of his hand at her back . . . He was tall and reedy and looked as if a stiff breeze might blow him over, but he was *strong*, as strong as her ex had been, she was certain, and he was leading her in an unspoken dance, securely enough that her toes needn't even touch the ground.

"So, do you work at the school?"

"I do. Just a few blocks away, actually." His deep voice was nearly a purr at her ear, a vibration she was able to feel down the side of her neck as he tipped his head to prevent her from needing to raise her voice. "The University is hosting my fellowship, and I'm doing some work with their agricultural study students in return. It's a very nice school, I've been in corporate labs that don't hold a candle. The research lab in the science facility is shockingly well-equipped for a school this size."

"Everything in Cambric Creek is shockingly well-equipped," she laughed in agreement, and realizing belatedly how that might be interpreted. She had no doubt that her Orcish and naga neighbors were indeed *well-equipped*, to say nothing about her Minotaurean coworker. *Probably even the satyr across the street*, she thought, ears burning. Grace considered the proximity of the University to her own house, realizing he had probably been coming home from work when he'd made the detour into her yard. "There's no shortage of funding around here, that's for sure. The community has deep pockets and they're not afraid to spend from them."

"I can tell. The neighborhoods are nothing like what I'm used to. The first apartment I looked at was on a street of these huge Victorians, and the house next door was a mansion!"

"Oldetowne," she nodded, flashing him a brilliant smile to encourage the conversation. He was more confident in the dark, his long fingered hand finding her with ease — her shoulder, her elbow, resting lightly at the small of her back. The weight of his red eyes never left her as she spoke, and the attention combined with his soft touch was making a giddy bubble of excitement swell in her chest. "Is that where you live?! Oh, no wait . . . you said you're over in the developments, right? By the woods?"

He clicked as he nodded his head, a curl of desire moving through her at the sound like a Pavlovian response.

"Literally in the woods, this family's property extends into the tree cover. Every other city I've lived in, it's been tiny little apartments with barely any trees . . . and here I'm in the forest with a solar-generator and retractable roof! I might be disgusted by the excess if I weren't currently enjoying it."

Grace laughed again, the sound bouncing off the stone walls of the circular building, earning another glare and huff from the lizard couple.

"I think they want us to be more serious," she'd giggled to him in a stage whisper as they moved around the observatory's dim interior.

"Too bad," he said lightly, pulling his arm free from hers to thread his long spindly fingers with her own. "*I'm* a scientist. They don't get to judge me. And this isn't a library." Grace giggled again, following him up the circular staircase to the door that would take them to the observation deck on the upper level. "Besides, science is supposed to be fun. Let's go outside."

The female half of the old lizard couple exclaimed in annoyance when the door pulled open, momentarily disrupting their work, before Merrick tugged her arm, pulling her outside and shutting the persnickety couple out.

"So are y-you from here?" he asked, once the heavy door had closed behind them. The evening was humid, and the gathering clouds to the east were an indication that the old lizard couple wouldn't be charting stars for much longer that night.

"No, I've only been here about three years. I'm from up-state, I moved here after I started working at the farm."

"Oh." He hesitated before continuing, a small fang appearing to worry at his thin lower lip. She grinned, silently marveling over how adorable his every gesture seemed to be. "Did-did you come here alone? When you moved? By-by yourself, I mean . . ."

He trailed off, a hint of his stammer making a return now that they were alone once more, the direction of the conversation more pointed. *Ah. Gotcha.* He was attempting to ascertain the lay of the land, and she realized he was probably wise to do so, chagrined that she'd not thought to do the same. After all, just because he stopped outside her bedroom window didn't mean he didn't have a wife and three children to fly home to, didn't mean he wasn't part-nered, coupled. Grace found it was suddenly very hard to swallow, her throat sticking. She had made the assumption that he was as single as her, and the notion that she might be mistaken made her stomach bunch and twist.

He watched you and it was probably like watching porn. Easy to disassociate. She didn't like to think she had performed in such a way for someone who *had* a someone waiting for him at home, but that would be typical. Far harder to brush aside whatever he'd done to suck on her clit in such a way. *Maybe that's why he's so nervous and awkward. There's a big difference between watching you orgasm and **helping** you orgasm. Here you are thinking he's just a sweet dork, and he's probably just twisting in guilt for having cheated.* She wondered if it was a partner he had at home or a spouse, if his life was perhaps as uncomplicated and easy to leave behind her own had been. *No children, no pets. No assets to divvy up.* The single joint banking account she and Tormand had shared had been used to pay household bills, and was not for savings. She'd simply turned off her direct deposit once she'd started making her plans, and that had been that. She wondered if this winged stranger was entangled in all of the trappings of partnership; all of the things people arbitrarily used as checkpoints for successful adult lives.

Since her move, she had all but lost contact with most of her friends from high school and university. Keeping up with them on social media was an exercise in self punishment, and even though nothing was ever said, Grace picked up on the superiority they felt in *having it all*. Every group text wound up being a conversation about their children, comparing brands of sippy cups and swim lessons, conversations to which she had nothing to contribute. Every DM asking how she was doing turned into a story about a family vacation or the PTA or some other topic to which she couldn't quite relate, utterly forgetting *they'd* reached out to *her*; her single, solitary life seeming inconsequential as a result. One of the things she loved most about her friend circle here in Cambric Creek was that Caleia and Ennika genuinely just liked hanging out. They wanted her to get laid, not married. Tula didn't care to discuss her kids in any way, shape, or form when they were out, and the work Grace did wasn't deemed as inferior just because she didn't have kids and a husband at home.

This is supposed to be a modern age, we're all supposed to be enlightened. Funny how they forget that.

She realized she'd not answered his question.

"I moved after my divorce, so yeah, alone. It's been nice, to be honest. We first got together when I was still in school, so this is the first time I've had to be an adult by myself."

"Why here? This doesn't seem like the sort of place a human would willingly choose."

Grace glanced up in surprise. She'd not had anyone second guess her move to Cambric Creek since her arrival, and she'd not been expecting the question. She was far from the only human in town, after all, and her friends didn't seem to hold her majority species status against her. *He's going to make you paranoid.*

"Work. I applied for the job when I saw the position, and I got it, which necessitated moving. Why do you ask?"

He shrugged with his free arm, raising his free hand in the air in a gesture of meh? "It's surprising to me that humans would *choose* to live here, where they're not . . ."

"In charge of everything?"

He grinned sheepishly, ducking his head. "I suppose that's one way to put it, yes. Where majority rule doesn't hold as much societal sway. I heard werewolves were in charge of this town. Your ex-husband was human?"

She didn't especially want to think about Tormand. She didn't want the memory of their relationship and the things she'd tolerated tainting her night, the way it had tainted six years of her life. She didn't want to speak of him or think of him at *all*, least of all to this adorable stranger, but she supposed she was the one who'd opened this door.

"No, he was a minotaur." His brow raised in response, surprise coloring his garnet eyes. "The area I'm from, it's not mixed species the way this place is, I've never lived anywhere like *this* before, but it was mixed enough, I guess? Humans are still the majority, of course, but . . . well, I didn't grow up in an all human town, not the way some people do."

"And your family was okay with that?"

"You say that like you are assuming they wouldn't have been."

He looked abashed for a moment, before shrugging again, a bit sheepishly. "I guess I am. I'm used to working with humans. When I say 'working with them' I mean working in the same lab, not actually *with* them. You keep to yourselves, mostly. Even if they respect you as a coworker or colleague, there's always a separation."

She frowned, disliking the knowledge that he'd been treated poorly by her kind, but knowing his words were true. There had never been a time in her life when she'd not been accepted or welcomed anywhere she went — she was the majority species, was the majority race within that species, and her life experience looked very different from those of her friends and neighbors. It was another reason why the property market in a place like Cambric Creek was likely so cutthroat. Her satyr and naga neighbors were insulated here, free from human majority, and the second-place status that came along with that majority.

"What about you? You just moved here this month, right? Are you here alone, or do you have like, seven little moth babies waiting for daddy to come home somewhere?"

He choked. Even the strangled sound that came from within that mound of fluff was adorable, she thought, grinning as he gasped and sputtered.

"N-no!" The horror in his voice made her laugh aloud, the sound swallowed up on the breeze. "Goddess no! I'm a scientist!" He threw up his free hand in a gesture of disbelief, the notion of him being coupled obviously one he couldn't fathom.

"What's that supposed to mean?! Scientists don't get to have love lives or families? Do you mean to tell me none of your co-workers are married?"

She had taken his arm again, almost unconsciously, mollified at his reaction to the question. The velvet of his skin was soft and sleek, and she would've been lying if she pretended she didn't want to feel its smoothness stretched across her entire body. As they drifted across the balcony, Grace tried to imagine what he would feel like above her, every inch of that plush sleekness pressed to her bare skin, his surprising weight sinking her into the mattress. She wondered how soft his velvet would feel against the inside of her thighs as she wrapped her legs around his narrow hips, pinned beneath his weight as he moved against her.

He shook his head ruefully. "Maybe, I don't know. I'm sure they exist, but they're smoother than me. No one wants to hear about hummingbirds and bats when they come home at night, and that's all I ever talk about."

Her unrestrained laughter echoed off the circular wall to their backs, and Grace was happy to note that for the first time, his smile was just as wide as hers.

"Well, *I* like bats and hummingbirds. I want to hear more about what you do."

His pointed little fangs gleamed white in the darkness, and she wondered if they would be sharp against the delicate skin of her throat, how they might scrape over the swollen buds of her nipples, trying to imagine them grazing her inner thighs. She was excited to go back to his place, she decided. *He's adorable and awkward, and if books and movies have taught us nothing else, it's always the cute nerdy guy who loves to eat pussy.* Grace blushed as she grinned, wondering if he'd notice the fire moving across her face, mirrored in the fire she felt spreading between her thighs at the thought of fangs against her skin. After all, hadn't she determined *that* was what had been missing from her fantasies about the big bull at work? She wanted to know what those little fangs would feel like nipping at the most sensitive parts of her, wanted him to do . . . whatever the fuck it was he'd done to her the last time, before his tongue made her see stars. *He nearly made you pass out and that was from outside the window!*

"I've never lived anywhere like this," he went on, oblivious to how wet she was making herself, just thinking about what they might do that night. "Like I said, I'm used to working with humans. Well," he corrected himself, "I'm used to being the only nonhuman in the lab, I guess that's more accurate to say. I very rarely work *with* people. And most of the time it didn't matter, because I was the only one coming in after normal working hours. Here I have to get used to actually having co-workers in the lab with me in the middle of the night."

Her mind was stuck in a quagmire of thick, grasping mud, unable to work out the meaning of his words for several beats. In the distance, thunder rumbled beyond the trees, and he clicked in disappointment at the sound, his brow furrowing as he looked out at the middle distance.

"We're not going to get to do much stargazing," he murmured mournfully, a sad little chirp punctuating his words. "I had the telescope set up for you and everything."

"Wait, what do you mean — are you . . . holy shit, are-are you nocturnal?" He blinked dolefully down at her, as if he weren't sure how he was meant to respond to her clearly idiotic question. There were other moth families in town, he was far from the only mothman Cambric Creek, several of whom patronized the farm regularly . . . and whom, she realized with dawning clarity, she'd never actually seen visit in the day.

There was a little family she was particularly fond of, husband and wife identical in their brown and orange markings, with wings bearing the great wide eyes of an owl, each wearing thick glasses. They had two small children, and Grace remembered the very first time she'd met them — their baby had been a fat, waving caterpillar, their little boy attempting mightily to hover off the ground on translucent, fledgling wings amongst the cornstalks. She had never seen them visit in the afternoons, had never greeted them at any of the daytime picnics or carnivals the farm hosted throughout the seasons . . . but she had seen them at her early morning table at the Maker's Mart, had smiled and waved the evening of the May Day fireworks. Each Saturday morning, local vendors and crafters set up tables in the community lot to peddle their wares, and she absolutely remembered them visiting the farm table, when the lot was still lit with hazy, early morning light. Merrick had shown up at the farm at dusk.

His jaw worked in what was likely another hard swallow, concealed by his mantle, and she was certain he would be flushing like a cherry if he were able. "Crepuscular, technically. I-I start my day in the evening, and I usually work overnight. I can come out in the day though," he said quickly, red eyes darting between the railing and her, as if he couldn't bear to make prolonged eye contact at that moment. "It's not like I turn to dust or anything. That's-that's actually what I study. The circadian rhythm of local pollinators and how they're disturbed by agricultural impacts. I would be able to come in and work during the day if I had to, the only adverse effects I might suffer would be crankiness." He paused, head cocking. "And that's everyone else's problem more than it would be mine," he added wryly, and she grinned again. "But when local pollinator populations are disturbed by agricultural and environmental stressors, it decreases their ability to effectively do their jobs. The animals suffer because they run into food scarcity issues they might not have otherwise, and crop diversity suffers without a robust pollinator community."

He continued to speak, his free hand dancing in the air to illustrate his increasingly complex points. Grace leaned on his arm as she grinned up at him, noting that he was easily able to support her weight without even shifting. His deep voice had evened out since the darkness had closed in around them, the slight stammer he possessed completely absent as he discussed his work, a confident edge replacing the chirping anxiety he had previously displayed. *Such a passionate, adorable dork.*

He cut off abruptly a few minutes later, mouth hanging open, his hand still suspended in the air. His fluffy antennae, which had been bobbing around as he spoke, now flattened to the side of his head, flush against his pointed ears.

"See," he laughed uncomfortably, lifting his shoulder in another self-deprecating, one-armed shrug, "this is why I'm single."

Adorkable. She was glad they'd moved outside, for she was unable to hold in her giggles, and she knew without a doubt the sour old reptilian couple would be huffing and puffing at her noisy display.

"So you used to be all alone in your old lab? Where was this?"

"Oh, all over. I've lived all over. Fellowships end, program funding is cut, research stipends are slashed . . . That usually means my position along with it. It's fine though, I'm used to it. And yes, usually alone. At least in the lab, at night. I have students this week though, first week in the classroom in over a year."

"Are you nervous?" she asked. "I would be a nervous wreck."

He chirped in response, in a tone that perfectly conveyed the wretchedness of the situation, and Grace found herself squeezing his forearm reassuringly, only catching herself after she had already done it.

"A bit. It's not my favorite part of the job, but it sometimes comes with the territory, that's the whole point of schools hosting the programs. I'm not a postdoc, otherwise I wouldn't have to. I usually know what to expect, you know, it's the same as it is in the labs. Humans . . ." he trailed off, swallowing again. "I know what to expect. Here though," another uneasy laugh and a small chirp, his antennae bobbing, "here I don't know what to expect. The first few nights coming in . . ." He broke off, his mantle puffing up as he clicked in aggravation, shaking his head. "The lab was full. Full! I've never had to make *conversation* like that at work. And they expected me to respond? To *talk* about myself?"

He made a small gurgle of exasperation, and Grace laughed again, easily able to imagine how out of his element he would be amongst the chatty coworkers of Cambric Creek. She'd quickly discovered that neighborhoods were close knit little enclaves, the people on your street like an extension of your family. Block parties and picnics were common occurrences, but that also meant that everyone was way too invested in everyone else's business. She had never lived in a place as fueled by gossip as Cambric Creek seemed to be.

She turned her face towards him as she giggled, burying her nose the briefest moment against his bicep. Silky smooth, as she expected. Grace inhaled deeply, breathing him in, attempting to commit his scent to memory. Warm and smokey, the smell of him reminded her of campfires at the lake; the scent of sharp, green sap and crunchy leaves in the underbrush, swirling around woodsmoke and embers and something cool — crisp and clean and begging her to press her lips against his soft, velutinous skin.

He hadn't been *leaving* work the nights he'd landed in her tree, she realized — he'd likely been just starting his day, waylaid by the erotic display she provided. Somehow, the thought that he had been on his way to his job when he stopped to watch her was even more mortifying, Grace thought. She wondered if he'd gone to work horny those nights, twisting in need from having watched her. Her fingertips dragged along his silky forearm, following the line of a raised tendon beneath his skin, her cunt pulsing when he shivered against her. Or he had reached completion from his place in the tree? Had he been jerking off as he watched her masturbate? She closed her eyes, biting her lip, trying to envision the scene. She knew who it was now; knew exactly who to envision. She wondered how he stroked himself, if he used a firm over-hand grip, or if he used both hands to stimulate his length, a cock she couldn't quite envision, not knowing enough about mothman anatomy to fill in the blanks on her own. Had he reached a messy climax, spattering the innocent leaves of her tree as he came? Or had he gone to work unfulfilled, his balls aching and full. *I wonder if he even has balls.*

She turned, trapping him against the iron railing that ringed the observation deck. That time, Grace was positive she was able to see the subtle movement of his throat, raising the thick ruff as he gulped. Her nose barely came to the center of his sternum, velvet coated and glowing silver-gray beneath the security lights, high above their head.

"So much for stargazing tonight," she echoed his earlier sentiment, carefully placing her hands against his bare chest as another roll of thunder shook the sky, not quite as far away now. He was just as silky smooth as she thought he would be, and it was all she could do to keep from grinding herself against his pelvis. *His balls are in his body, with his cock.* Like so many of her nonhuman neighbors, his anatomy was designed in such a way that his reproductive organs were safe from external harm. It seemed like an evolutionary plus, but it didn't do much for her in the moment. *You'll just have to tease them out.*

"S-stupid weather."

"Why don't you wear clothes?" It felt like too personal a question to be asking, but he hadn't hesitated to ask her personal questions. At first glance last night, she had thought him reed-thin and wispy, but now that she was up close and personal, it was easy to see the way his height and large wings made him seem skinnier than he truly was. He was lithe and sinewy but his shoulders were broad, and his chest hard beneath her hands. She dragged her fingertips slowly down the wide expanse of smooth velvety skin, pausing at his ribs, feeling his lungs hitch. His breathing was hard, his chest rising and falling rapidly beneath her palms, breath ragged when his thin lips parted.

"They make flying hard. The last place I lived, not the city, the place before that, I was studying bats in their natural habitats and the only transportation up the mountain every day was a convoy of jeeps. They made two trips up and two trips down, and all of those occurred in the daytime. Flying was the only way to get anywhere. And clothes don't last very long against the wind."

"Everything here is walkable," she murmured with a smile, stroking his pectorals once more. "And there's good public transportation. But I didn't even think about flying. Not that I have any complaints, mind you, but it might help you fit in better. But," she added with a sly smile, "you don't have to wear them around me. I could get used to the lack of barriers. Do you want to come back to my place for a bit?"

Once more, desire outran her good sense. Her palm slid down his front, slowing as she dragged over his taut abdomen, coming closer and closer to the place where his most sensitive anatomy must be held. Her fingers had just found the start of a slight dip in his skin when he gripped her wrist, preventing her from moving any further. He was panting by then. Grace was certain she would be able to sit on the floor and lift her legs and slide her way home, she was so wet and ready to have him in her bed. *He's sweet and adorable and we're going to fuck him into next month.*

"Do you want to come back to my place?" she repeated pointedly, not moving the hand that he still gripped. She wondered what it would take to rouse his cock from his hiding place, and she intended on finding out. "I know you said you have some work to do, but . . . maybe just for a bit?" *Just long enough to fuck, at least once.*

"Yes." His voice was a low scrape, the desire she heard in it vibrating against her chest, but his grip on her wrist did not relax. "But I shouldn't."

She pushed up onto her toes, the strong, solid length of him supporting her. He was so tall, she was still not quite able to reach his mouth, but he was able to feel the heat of her breath, clicking as he panted.

"Why not?" she whispered.

For a long moment, the only sound with his ragged breath and the increasing thunder of the approaching storm. They needed to leave soon, before the sky opened above them, but first she wanted an answer. His mouth quirked up slightly, his antennae dancing.

"You're not one of those human women who likes to play bedroom bingo with other species, are you?"

Her mouth dropped open in shock, not expecting such a straightforward accusation from her bashful-seeming, stammering companion, but before she had a chance to feel mortified, both of her hips were locked in his iron grip as he pulled his body, holding her securely. His thin mouth was warm as it pressed to hers, and the thumb that pressed circles into her hips was rhythmic in its movement. Grace traced the shape of his thin, nearly non-existent lips with the tip of her tongue, and when she pressed into the hot cavern of his mouth, he purred against her, his twilight-colored wings vibrating in a frenzy. She had wondered over the texture of the mantle around his neck, and as she sunk gripping fingers into its pile, she wondered no longer. Incredibly soft, almost silky in texture and impossibly thick, she desperately wanted to know what it would be like to wake up with her bare body pressed to his, her face resting against this mound of fluffy softness. He pulled back far too quickly for her liking, lowering her gently back to the ground. Grace realized she hadn't even been aware her feet were dangling in the air, so secure his grip had been.

"For your information, Mr. Nosy, I haven't even been involved with anyone since I moved here. Are you one of those nonhumans who just likes dabbling in smaller species? Don't mothmen abduct women off bridges?"

"That's an urban legend, actually," he answered matter-of-factly, ignoring her outraged laughter. "And being a smaller species doesn't have anything to do with it."

"Did you like watching me?" She was enjoying the hammering of his heartbeat against her, even enjoyed the way he squirmed at the question. *He liked it enough that he came back.*

"Yes," he breathed, not bothering to deny it.

She would be shocked at herself in the morning, Grace knew, but that didn't matter at the moment. She felt as brave as she'd been those two nights when she performed for him desperately wanting to tease him into action.

"Do you want to have another taste?" His groan against her was a rumble that went straight to her cunt, seeming to vibrate against her clit.

"Yes," he wheezed. "And that's why I shouldn't come over tonight."

Grace opened her mouth to protest, but the storm had arrived. Another rumble of thunder, accompanied by fat rain droplets spattering the concrete platform. It was a matter of minutes before the sky opened on them, all the better reason for him to come back to her house.

"But I-I'd like to see you again? If you'd like to? That is, if I didn't scare you off with all the bats and hummingbirds."

She wasn't interested in dating, didn't want to spend an inordinate amount of time playing the let's get to know each other game, not when all she wanted was to find out how good he could make her feel, if he fucked as well as he sucked . . . but he was too sweet and adorable to say no to, she thought ruefully. Now she understood what men so often meant when they said they were taken in by kittenish looks and batting eyelashes. The nervous antennae flattened around his head were enough to make her say yes to anything he wanted.

"I'd like that. Maybe this weekend?"

Sure enough, the rain was pelting down by the time they left, the lizard couple long gone. She squealed, running the short distance from the observatory to her car, hunched under the protective cover of his wide wings.

"I'll call you this weekend?" He asked hesitantly, hunching at her window, his garnet eyes full of hope, heedless of the water that ran in rivulets down the sloped planes of his high cheekbones. They'd exchanged numbers in the building, and her stomach had flip-flopped again, typing his name into her phone. *Merrick*. It seemed oddly permanent, a ridiculous notion, but one she was unable to push away.

"That sounds perfect." She grabbed at his hand before he was able to pull away from her window, that bubble of warmth in her chest not diminishing. "Good luck this week with your students. I'm sure you'll do great. And try to make some friends. You're not in an all human town anymore."

She leaned up, pushing her face through the open window until she was able to reach the corner of his mouth. Grace felt his breath stutter against her lips as she kissed him gently, the adorable chirp that came from his throat sending a lick of desire down her back. *This weekend. We're going to tie him to the bed if we have to this weekend*. A glance into her rearview mirror showed him still standing there, frozen in place as she pulled out of the parking lot, a long-fingered hand raised in parting.

She hung the soaking wet dress on the back of her bathroom door when she got home, slipping into a short cotton nightgown, and attempted not to think about how he managed to reignite the fire beneath her skin with his every adorable sound and gesture. *I wonder what kind of sounds he'll make when I try to suck his soul through his cock.* Grace was certain he wasn't even her type. He was too nice, too sweet and shy . . . *Wait, why isn't that your type? How do you even know what your type is? You went from dating humans to marrying a minotaur, with no in between. Are you saying assholes are your type?* He was nothing like Torm, that was for certain. He wasn't much like anyone else she'd ever dated either . . . but, she considered, that wasn't a bad thing.

It wasn't until she was stretched out beneath her sheets that she realized her arms were lightly covered in a soft grey powder. She had a moment of panic, thinking it was something from the old observatory's ceiling, when she realized with a jolt that it had come from his wings, as he'd tented them over her. She gently stroked her fingertips against her arm, a trace of his soft velvet left behind, a new element to her fantasies. Rolling to her side, she leaned over to the bedside table, burying her nose in the small vase she'd placed there, inhaling the soft floral scent of the little bouquet. *A return to happiness.*

Grace flopped against her pillows, closing her eyes briefly, still trailing her fingers over the velvet powder he'd left behind before reaching back to the bedside table and opening the drawer. *Too horny to think.* It wasn't the way she'd hoped to spend the night, turning on her vibrator to check the battery power, but she'd not be able to sleep until she quenched the fire his soft, awkward chirps had ignited. *This weekend.* She wasn't looking for love, she reminded herself, settling back against her pillows. That didn't explain why the weekend seemed so interminably far away, she thought just before the whirring motor the vibrator obliterated her thoughts, the closest approximation to the buzzing of his wings she could manage.

CHAPTER FIVE

Five

"The main thing is really to just think of everything. Plan for every eventuality, and you'll be fine. Don't overthink it, it's that simple. But of course, you already know that. If you were able to do the Millbreen wedding, this will be like a walk in the park."

Grace rolled her eyes. She hadn't pulled away for the afternoon to have her own job's high-level description parroted back at her, yet here she was, not bothering to hide her disdain for her companion's elementary advice.

"Wow, that's really illuminating. Thank you so much for meeting me today to give me that little nugget of wisdom, Tris. Truly I never, ever would have figured that out without your sage words of advice. I'll be sure to stop into the city council meeting this month when you explain that water is, in fact, wet." The satyr across the table grinned broadly, giving her a little wink. His cherub-like curls tumbled over his forehead, grazing the bridge of his nose, and she clenched her hands into fists to keep from leaning across the table and pushing them out of his face. His name was Tris, and Grace had known the cocky bastard for years.

People like Tris existed on the periphery of every elite social circle. Attendees at every party, somehow securing invites to the most exclusive of soirées without fail, like a Greek chorus moving at the edges of friend groups and families and people who typically only had two things in common: power and money. They never seemed to be related to anyone of any social importance or hold any jobs that made the engines of commerce hum, but they were always there, always present, until the thought of having a function and not inviting them was simply not considered.

He was a gossip columnist, a profession that fit him to a T, she thought. She had first met him at a wedding she'd planned — the daughter of a local politician, whose country club nuptials had been canceled at the last-minute due to an overbooking. By the time Grace had been brought in to manage the affair, everything that could have gone wrong already had. It had been up to her to smooth ruffled feathers, to restore order, and to turn an existing cluster fuck into a storybook happy ending and she did so with a smile. Tris had been a guest, an acquaintance of someone or another. He'd been hazy on the details of exactly who it was he had known, but he possessed an invitation, an easy gift of the gab, and more importantly, a flask of top shelf whiskey in the inner pocket of his impeccably tailored jacket. When he'd proffered it to her, she hadn't hesitated, and his number had gone into her file of contacts, as someone who knew everyone. Florists and caterers, hall owners and country club directors; anyone who was anyone who had anything to offer was someone with whom he was acquainted, and by Grace being acquainted with *him*, she was, by dint, acquainted with everyone.

She'd been shocked to find him in Cambric Creek, running into him for the first time in years at the same place where they now sat, the Black Sheep Beanery, the busiest business in town. Tris, for his part, hadn't seemed that surprised.

"The wheel always comes around, darling. Everyone you know will eventually wind up in some other place, and someday, you will too."

A laughing trio approached their table from the pickup counter — a towering orc who was handsome enough to grace billboards in his underwear, and two human-looking women, one in a lab coat and the other in scrubs.

"Hold on, the new doctor gets a Danish!" The ewe-faced woman who owned the coffee shop had followed the group down the aisle, brandishing a paper bag she handed to the young woman in the lab coat, the girl's glasses slipping down her nose as her head dipped bashfully.

"What does that make me, chopped gizzards?"

The sheep woman's beaming smile never left her face as she rolled her eyes at the chuckling orc.

"That makes you a private practice doctor who can afford to pay for his coffee, Kanar."

The trio took the table behind them as Tris returned her eye roll with a dazzling smile of his own, sipping at his tea.

"Really, it's just a little community planning committee. I don't know what you're worried over. If it's raining, have an umbrella. If it's hot, offer her something cold to drink. I don't need to tell you how to plan your event, that's what you *do*, Gracie. The point is to let her see that you are prepared for any outcome, meaning their little festival will be in good hands."

She had already bought weights for the tables, and would make sure they were secured to the legs of her own before the werecat who headed the committee arrived for their meeting, in the event of a never-before-seen windstorm. She would have sparkling water and flat, had already purchased a case of sparkling elderflower lemonade, and would rim the glass in the farm's own honey — a sweet, refreshing reminder of the bounty that Saddlethorne provided the community.

"Honestly, you should be glad it's Greta. Sandi would've put you through the gulag. Speaking of which," he raised a caramel-colored eyebrow meaningfully, "I would make sure your political affiliation is on clear display, if you know what I mean. The were community is putting up a united front, and it'll make them happy to know Saddlethorne is a part of that."

She waved away the suggestion, taking another sip of her coffee. The Beanery was a vital hub of connections — the entire town passed through its doors on a weekly basis and she knew if she ever had trouble pinning someone down or getting them on the phone, she would be able to stake out the coffee shop and run into them eventually.

"I don't know what I can do about that. I have no idea who Cal is planning on voting for. What am I supposed to do, have 'Hemming for Mayor' signs lining the drive?"

"Well, I wouldn't go quite that far, but at least one wouldn't hurt. Street-level, so people can see it when they're coming up the road. Shout it loud and proud."

"But I really don't know if —"

"It doesn't matter, Grace." Tris leaned over the table, his thick tumble of curls falling around his horns. From a distance, he gave the impression of being at least a decade younger than he was, but from her current vantage point only inches away, she was reminded that he'd been around the block — around and around and around — for years, and that she'd be wise to take his advice. After all, she reminded herself with a sigh, that was the whole point in meeting with him today. Tris was a valuable asset, and she wasn't about to turn her nose up at his knowledge and opinions.

"Cal is free to vote for whoever he wants to, come elections. It's a private booth, no one needs to go in with him. But *Saddlethorne* should be advertising their support. Especially if *you* want to contract like *this*. Like I said, the entire were community is united. The cats, wolves, bears, all of them. Shifters too. You don't want to be on the wrong side of this one, trust me."

Grace scowled. She didn't like having to play games involving local politics, and wanted the business to stand on its own merits, using the talking points she'd painstakingly developed over the past three years. Worst of all, she knew he was right. She wanted this contract badly, wanted it for Cal and the farm and the business it would bring him, that recognition of being a community landmark in a dying profession. More than that, she was forced to admit, she wanted it for herself — tangible proof that she was good at her job, that she had earned her place in the community and wasn't just another human moving in because she wanted to fuck the neighbors. She wasn't there just to experience a non-human dating pool, and she didn't want people to assume she was. She wanted this planning community contract, and that meant she couldn't afford to be making enemies with the committee itself.

That Jackson Hemming would be elected as the town's new mayor come November was a foregone conclusion. The Hemming family had, after all, been at the forefront of Cambric Creek since the town's inception. Mayors, judges and magistrates, town treasurer, city officials both elected and appointed — if there was a position of power to be had in Cambric Creek, odds were good a Hemming had held it at one point, and would do so again in the future.

The future, it seemed, was here, and Grace knew Tris was right. If she wanted to be the planning committee's official venue for future events, it wouldn't do to have Cal running off at the mouth about how much he liked the incumbent candidate. She had no idea how Cal felt, nor how he was planning on voting, but that in and of itself was a bit damning.

Everywhere she went in town, people fawned over the handsome werewolves, and the fact that Cal had never voiced
an opinion on the family's return to political power didn't
bode well. She pressed her mouth in a flat line and huffed,
aggravated that Tris was right, but unable to deny it.

"Fine, I'll get a sign. At the road, like you said. Right in sight
of all that southbound traffic on weekends. Is there anything
else you can tell me about Greta? Anything *actually* helpful?

The handsome satyr smirked, making a great show of sipping his tea once more. "Gracie, I don't know what you're so
worked up over. It's a stupid little festival. You're the biggest
farm in town. Where else are they going to go? The winery?
Enoch would run them off before they even had a chance
to put on their brand-new equestrian boots and designer
sweaters. Fucking relax, will you?"

She listened as attentively as she was able as Tris chattered
on for the next thirty minutes or so, but she found it impossible to fully concentrate on her companion's conversation.
Every few minutes she would flip over her phone, checking to
see if she had any missed notifications, double checking the
volume to make sure she'd not turned it off, triple checking
that she'd not accidentally swiped on the 'do not disturb'
feature.

"Am I keeping you from something? I can't tell if you're
checking the time or if you're expecting a call, but in either
case, if you need to get going . . ." The satyr raised his hand,
gesturing towards the door, and she flushed, knowing she
was being rude.

"Sorry, no I don't need — I don't have anywhere to be. Everyone knows I had a work lunch today, I have someone running my table. They can do without me for the afternoon."

Tris leaned over the table, eyes sparkling, and Grace realized that she'd made a terrible mistake.

"So if it's not the time you're checking, then it's a message. A message you've not yet received, but one you're waiting for on pins and needles. Let's see . . . you've already established you're away for the afternoon and you have everything at work covered, so it's not a message from the farm. The only bit of business concerning you right now is this harvest festival contract, which is the whole point of us meeting here today, so we can safely assume it's not work-related."

"Actually, we have a lot of catching up to—" She attempted to redirect, but Tris paid her no mind, barreling on as if she'd not spoken at all.

"And if it's not work related, then it must be personal. Your family lives a distance away, and if anyone were sick or in hospital, I can't imagine you would be taking the time to shoot the breeze with me today and not go rushing to their side, or at least you would've told me about it when you arrived, just in case an emergency phone call necessitated you stepping away. I specifically remember you saying you were an only child—"

"When," she cut in, having no recollection of having such a conversation with the smug satyr. "When would I have ever told you that?"

"Five years ago, 50th anniversary party at the Selsby Yacht Club," he shot back without missing a beat. "The Bristol sisters had a catfight in the coatroom and you said it was moments like that when you were glad to be an only child, right before one of them toppled into the chocolate fountain."

Grace sat back, chagrined. Tris was a valuable acquaintance, she reminded herself. He knew everyone and his mind was like a steel trap for details, but the same attributes that made him valuable also made him dangerous. He never forgot a thing.

So it's not work and it's not family, that means you've either found time for a hobby, or you're fucking someone new." He sat back smugly, the sparkle in his eye telling her that he absolutely did not believe she had somehow found time for a hobby. "Gracie, I do believe you owe me a little something. Who is he?"

He didn't bother stating it as a question, and she heard the demand for what it was. She withered in her seat, wondering why it was that the whole town came to this coffee shop, day in and day out, knowing everyone else was there to watch them living their lives in public. Far better to be invisible, she thought. *Big words for an exhibitionist.* She could never let Tris know about the way she and Merrick had met, not unless she wanted every last resident of Cambric Creek to know she regularly masturbated in front of her open window for audiences by the following afternoon.

"I'm not actually fucking anyone." He cocked an eyebrow in sly disbelief. "I went out on a date the other night, he's new in town. A mothman. He's a scientist, works at the school." She didn't bother holding back, because she knew if Tris wanted to find out, he would root out the information before she'd even crossed the Black Sheep's parking lot. "We've only been out that one time, and I thought we were going to make plans for this weekend, but I haven't heard from him yet. There. Are you happy now?"

He tutted. "These men act like boys, and then they wonder why they're treated like infants in their relationships. If you haven't heard from him by Thursday, delete his number. You're too good for that."

"I don't know if I'm actually all that interested in the dating part of it, to tell you the truth."

His laughter had the sharp ring of a bell, and he leaned across the table conspiratorially once more.

"If all you're looking for is a little fucky fucky, that's easy to find. If you're in the market for a horny partner, I'll compile you a list. This town has no shortage of them. You know, you humans get a bad rap for this sort of thing, but there's at least three folks on every block hungry to bury their giant—"

The Orcish doctor at the table behind them stood abruptly, a phone call from the hospital ending their coffee break short, necessitating his companions to stand as well, to let him out. "I may as well go back with you," the human doctor sighed, the girl in scrubs groaning her agreement. When Grace turned back to Tris, he was still talking.

"—tight little human holes. So say the word, if you want to list."

Grace glared. "Let me guess, your name will be at the top of said list."

Tris grinned widely, gesturing to his lap beneath the table. "I'm a satyr. If I weren't horny all the time, I would just be a goat, Grace."

She squirmed in her seat, thinking of her neighbor and the far from innocent neighborly thoughts she'd had. *See, it's probably a good thing this all happened and Merrick landed outside your window. Otherwise you really would've ended up with the horny satyr across the street.* "What about you," she challenged. "What have you been up to? You have to tell me, now that you made me tell you mine."

He chuckled, cracking his knuckles and rolling his shoulders. The coffee shop was now packed, and they needed to vacate their table. It was just as well, she thought. She needed to get back, needed to corner Cal and give him the third degree over Jackson Hemming and whether or not he was going to let her put out a sign at the street.

"I know this will shock you, but I'm not currently involved with anyone." Grace rolled her eyes, and Tris scoffed. "Not seriously. Don't get me wrong, I've been fucking a beautiful little half-shifter, Sulya Slade's second cousin's brother-in-law's daughter, or something like that. But it's hardly a relationship." His smile stretched, his eyes glimmering like diamonds, those ridiculous curls tumbling over his forehead once more. "I'm pretty sure she hates me, actually. Which just makes it more fun."

Grace gathered her things, pushing up from the table. "You are literally the worst person I know, Tris. Don't ever change."

She'd only been back at Saddlethorne for a few minutes, when she decided she'd made a mistake in returning that day at all. The goblin from the farmstand who'd been covering duty on her table had practically fled the moment she returned, mumbling about the unbearable heat and the non-stop parade of snot-nosed brats that afternoon. She rolled her eyes, taking her place behind the welcome table, powering on her tablet, and stared out at . . . nothing. The parking lot was empty. Whatever shoppers had been in earlier, the heat of the day had effectively frightened them all off, leaving her to bake beneath her umbrella alone.

It wasn't long before Caleia sought her out, dragging dramatically across the concrete until she reached the table, dropping into a chair with a groan. "We shouldn't even be open today, it's too fucking hot. No one is coming out in this heat. You should tell Cal it's a waste of payroll to be here."

"At least not this afternoon," Grace agreed. "We might pick up again in the evening, but you're right. No one is coming out in this right now. But *I'm* not telling Cal anything."

"How did your gossip lunch go? Did he have any sneaky insight on what we can do to impress them?"

Grace dropped back in her chair, head lolling. She scowled at the interior of the umbrella, thinking of Tris and his nosy questions. "Not really. Well, yes and no. He confirmed everything I already suspected — they want to know that the festival will be in good hands and they don't need to step in and worry about any of the details, and we'll be fine on that. Details are what I do. But then he also had a suggestion to butter them up that I don't think Cal is going to like very much."

She'd only just said the words, when the telltale clip-clop of the big centaur's approach reverberated off the concrete. Grace raised her head, able to immediately ascertain that something was wrong. Cal was taciturn and gruff and while she'd been intimidated by his briskness at first, she quickly learned that was his default state, and a bark was pretty much all he had. Now though, she could tell he'd been grumbling, his fingers snapping in agitation. Grace wondered if it was worth asking what had set him off, when he addressed them first.

"We've got company tomorrow," he snapped, hooves stamping the ground in annoyance. "So we need to make sure this place looks 'hospitable'."

She surveyed the space at Cal's words: cheery red and white gingham graced the tables for the visitors and CSA inquiries, the pavement was swept, the lawn neatly edged. Rustic, hand lettered signs advertising the pick-your-own produce fields and hand crafted cheeses were hung on the bright red barn, and there was a spit-shine on the green tractor that was kept parked on the edge of the pavement.

"Cal, my house isn't even this neat," she pointed out as Caleia harrumphed indignantly at the centaur's insinuation.

"And I don't have anything on the books for tomorrow. What's going on?"

"Those busybodies from the horticulture department at the university, they're working with some scientists on making the community farms more 'hospitable' for local pollinators. They're sending some labcoat know-it-all out to talk with us and old man Mills up the road tomorrow. I talked to the guy for three minutes and I'm already pissed off. Real patronizing, I can already tell."

A shiver moved up her spine, despite the sweltering heat. *He would have told you if he was coming back to the farm, right?* She'd not been lying when she'd told Tris she had nearly given up on the bashful moth man. She texted him the following evening, after their observatory date, wishing him luck with his students that week, and she'd not heard from him since. Now the weekend loomed, just another day and a half away, and they'd still not made plans. Grace didn't like the way her stomach twisted when she considered that he simply wasn't that into her, reminding herself that she really ought not to care. *So you find someone else to hook up with, whatever.* But the notion of him coming back to Saddlethorne now, without even mentioning it to her . . . Her hands clenched into fists at her side, and she waited until Cal had cantered away before pulling out her phone, jabbing the screen in annoyance.

Are you a labcoat know-it-all?

It shouldn't have been surprising when hours passed before her phone buzzed with his response. The mid-day sun had been high in the sky when she sent the message, a bead of sweat dropping from the frizzy halo of curls that had escaped her bun, and more than just a bead of aggravation heating her neck. Her lunch with Tris hadn't taken nearly as long as she could have made it, and she regretted returning at all to hear the news that she'd been blown off.

Somewhere across town, she reminded herself, in a rental unit he said was literally in the woods, he was asleep. Grace wondered *how* he slept. Stretched out like a giant, winged beast, his long limbs fully extended in his wings rest, wide and enormous? Perhaps he curled into a ball of fluff, his puffy mantle serving as a pillow he snuggled into, wings wrapped around himself. Each option was more adorable than the last, she was forced to admit, annoyed all over again. When the phone finally buzzed at the edge of the table, her stomach flip-flopped, her heart rate kicking up a few notches. She gripped the edge of the table, counting to ten before she reached out for her phone.

I actually just put my lab coat on

And now that you mention it, people have called me a know-it-all

So . . . yes?

Grace tipped her head back, closing her eyes. It was late afternoon, and the sky was still a brilliant Azure. She wondered if he just woken up, if his soft velvet was rumpled from sleep, still puffed up and standing on end. The thought made her smile. Against her better judgment, she still hoped she would get to determine whether or not the notion had any truth. She wanted to learn how he slept, see his face smoothed out and relaxed; wondered if his constantly bobbing antennae would be at rest. This wasn't one of her long evenings and she would be packing up to go home soon, back to her own little rental house on Persimmon Street, where the tree outside her window was in full cover, obscuring her from the view of her neighbors in the street below. Back to her little house, on the route one would take if one were going to the biology lab at the University.

Are you the lab coat know-it-all coming to the farm tomorrow?

She ought not to care, Grace reminded herself. She wasn't looking for a relationship or love; she only sought to soothe the itch beneath her skin. She ought not to care, but she undeniably did, and she couldn't keep denying that fact. She had been twisting all week long in the absence of his call, wondering if she would see him again, if she would get to hear those adorable little chirps and clicks. If she didn't care, she could have moved on to something or someone else at that point, but the fact remained that she *did* care. Against her better judgment she had begun caring, and it was far too late to unring the bell now.

How am I supposed to surprise you if you already know about that

Hey, wait

Is that what he called me?!

Grace grinned, that same giddy bubble of warmth rising on beating wings in her chest once more. He was coming tomorrow, and he had wanted to surprise her. Even though he had kept her twisting in the wind for the better part of the week, since that night at the observatory. Her phone buzzed again before she had a chance to respond.

If people snatch away my surprises, what do I have left?

We've already been through this, I'm not that smooth

At that she laughed out loud. He was adorable.

Someone told me that even scientists get to have love lives and families.

I've not yet tested that hypothesis, but I figured there was only one way to find out

She knew she ought to listen to her own good advice, but that didn't prevent her smile from stretching widely at the thought of seeing him the following night, of holding his strong hand and hearing his soft chirps. Her phone buzzed once more, vibrating against the red and white checkered tablecloth.

Besides, a beautiful little birdie told me the blackberries would be ripe this week

And she needs to help me pick them

CHAPTER SIX

Six

*I*n . . . *two* . . . *three* . . .

She held the slowly inhaled breath for several beats, attempting to focus on the still air, thick with the day's heat, and the encroaching twilight. The sun had blazed across the sky for a second afternoon, giving a perfect excuse for the little slip dress she wore, probably too revealing for the workplace, she considered, once again thankful for the lack of an HR department, but easily overlooked with the balmy weather. It had *nothing* to do with the farm's evening visitor.

Out . . . *two* . . . *three* . . .

"What are you still hanging around for? I can give you a lift if you're having car trouble?"

The sky was a wash of violet, thready fingers of pale pink slowly receding as the sun sank into the trees. Brogan's hulking form cast a wide shadow in the dying light, completely engulfing the outline of her own on the gravel.

She turned, giving the big minotaur a smile before shaking her head. "No, I'm not stranded . . . but thank you."

"Working late?"

"I . . . need to talk with Cal. I booked a last-minute wedding today and it's coming up fast, so it might be all hands on deck getting things ready for a few days."

As soon as the words were out, Callum's voice rose stridently, cutting across the distant field and interrupting the serene chirping of the crickets. This was the fourth or fifth time he'd done so, and she could only imagine the aggravation with which the terse centaur argued his point, whatever it may have been. The low hum of Merrick's deep voice could not be heard from this distance, and she suspected that even if he deigned to shout back at the centaur, which she couldn't imagine the soft-spoken moth doing, the sound would still be too low to hear.

Behind her, Brogan snorted. "Can't imagine he's going to be in a chatty mood after this. These lab types always think they know more than anyone else . . . What are we going to need for this, the hall barn? I'll have a few of the boys empty it out first thing in the morning, shouldn't take too long. The banquet tables are still in there, you just need to tell them what you want left. Are you going to want the floors rewaxed?"

Grace breathed a small sigh of relief, turning to her big co-worker with a smile. They had all been somewhat perplexed when she'd started, unsure of what her role would be and if it would mean changes for everyone, and it

had, to some extent. Everyone's position became somewhat public-facing as she booked in school tours and bus
trips, agri-tourism being a growing sector of the burgeoning
lifestyle business. They'd had to hire more employees, had
requisitioned one of the barns as a rental hall, a construction
project that extended it and made it gleam, comfortably
able to hold a medium-sized wedding reception. The existing
farm employees had to learn to keep their cursing restricted
to areas where guests would not hear them, and they'd all
become actors, in some small measure . . . and they'd all
embraced it, eager to smile and wave to school children and
explain their jobs to busloads of seniors, there to tour the
facilities and have a farm-to-table lunch.

"That would be amazing, thank you. Yeah, we'll probably
need to wax. Let's see, it's a guestlist of one hundred and
fifty, so that's seven tables, one for the bridal party, two for
catering . . . let's leave out fourteen just to be safe."

"Sounds good, they'll get it done in the morning. I hate
leaving you out here in the dark. I could wait, if you want to
get a drink or someth—"

"I have plans," she interrupted quickly. "If they're not
wrapped up in a few, I'll probably get going myself . . . see
you tomorrow, yeah? And thanks again."

The big bull cocked his head curiously, hesitating before saying goodnight, and she turned back to face the
field, listening for the crunching gravel signifying his retreat.
Co-workers were tricky, and she'd not spoil the delicate fabric
of her life at Saddlethorne. Brogan had already expressed

his *appreciation* for her dress, sidling up to her table as he passed to pointedly remind her that he had no intention of being unprofessional at work, but if she should feel inclined to meet him at the storage barn in the back field for an off-the-clock lunch break, he'd show her just how appreciative he was.

"It's a waste to spend the whole day sitting under this umbrella," he'd breezed, leaning on the shovel he carried. "You ought to take a walk, get away from the table for a bit. Find a bit of shade in the storage barn."

"I have shade under my umbrella," she'd pointed out as he'd chuckled. "No sense in working up a sweat traipsing across the fields."

"There are better ways we can work up a sweat, Grace. That far away, you could moan as loud as you want, no one would hear you."

It was somewhat galling to admit to herself that two short weeks ago, the temptation of being railed by her barrel-chested co-worker in the middle of the day, far enough from the main part of the farm that no one would hear her screams of pleasure, might have been too great to ignore. *Too horny to think . . .*

"I'm not wearing my traipsing shoes today. And besides, you need to get a move on if you're going to be back from break before Cal wants to have his meeting." When he'd cocked his head questioningly, she'd given him a beatific smile. "What if there's a backup at the milking place? You want to give them time to drain every last drop."

His chuckle had bounced off the interior of her umbrella, trapping her in its rumble. "Oh don't you worry, there's no danger of a dairy shortage here." She held her breath as he adjusted himself, lifting his huge testicles from where they were confined in his snug jeans. Squeezing her thighs together, she tried to look unaffected. "You need to have a glass sometime, Grace. This milk does a body good."

The sound of his pickup rumbling to life now silenced the crickets one more, leaving her alone in the still, growing darkness. Despite the fact that she was practically holding her breath in an effort to hear the two men out in the field, the resumed night chorus of crickets and frogs was all that met her. When a light at Callum's house flared to life in the distant darkness, she realized their meeting was over. *He left. He left without even saying hello or goodbye.*

She'd been signing up a couple for the CSA program when Merrick arrived that evening. Callum had met him at the visitor's table before she'd had a chance to breakaway, although from across the wide concrete pad she'd watched the tall centaur assess the equally tall moth. To his credit, Merrick seemed unfazed by Cal's brusqueness, meeting his outstretched hand coolly before the two had trooped off to an outer field without a backwards glance.

The text message had come shortly after the couple had left her table, happy with their new produce subscription and heading off to the farmstand shop at her encouragement. When she saw Tris's name, her stomach swooped, expecting something about the community contract she wanted so badly. She'd not expected it to be about the tall, bashful moth man she was seeing that night.

I don't know if you ever heard from your new friend
But he's had five different addresses in the last four years
Here for a good time, but not a long time
Who cares if he's trash, I say make the most of it

He'd told her he lived all over. He'd *not* mentioned that he didn't stay in place for very long. Grace couldn't quite explain why her stomach had tightened and clenched as she read and reread the text message, over and over again. Hadn't she been telling herself for the past week that she didn't want a relationship? That she wasn't looking for love? Why then should it matter? *Because you liked him. He's the first person you've actually liked in a long time. And now he's gone.* Suddenly she felt ridiculous in the flimsy sundress, for the way she'd taken extra care with her hair that morning, for the berry-colored lip gloss she'd worn. *He's not interested and you're a fool.*

A low thrumming was the only indication that she was wrong. The buzzing of a high-voltage wire, growing in intensity as her head whipped around in the gathering darkness, the sound only just registering when Merrick suddenly appeared before her, dropping from the sky in a graceful landing, making her shriek in surprise.

"Sorry," he gasped, gripping her by the shoulders as she wobbled on the gravel. His antennae danced in the lamplight as she reeled, red eyes peering down in concern. Surprise quickly gave way to pealing laughter, and once she started it was impossible to stop, leaning into his strong arms as she shook with mirth. He could claim it was an urban legend all he wanted, the way he'd appeared like some giant winged menace was more than just a bit disconcerting. *No wonder humans make up stories!*

"I-I got turned around out in the field, and I didn't want to be walking around lost all night if you were waiting. I-I wasn't sure if you were, I thought you might have left, but I didn't want to keep you if—"

It wasn't easy hauling him down to her, but somehow she managed, silencing his adorable stammer with her lips, needing to feel his heat and smell the warm, smokey smell of him to banish her insecurities. It worked, particularly when long, tapered fingers buried in her hair, his small fangs catching her lower lip as she broke off the kiss.

"How'd you get lost?" she gasped, nuzzling her cheek against his fluffy mantle before dropping down from her toes. "Did you wander into the corn or something?"

His smile was grim, and red eyes flickered to the light out in the distance. "Your boss told me to hang a left at the mouth of the corn. I knew it wasn't the way we'd come in, but I naively thought he was sending me on a shortcut."

"To the left of the corn field? But that's—" She clapped a hand over her mouth to hold in another wave of laughter as Merrick shook his head disdainfully. "That's the pig enclosure! Callum, you old goat!"

"I smelled them before I got too close, fortunately. Quite a charmer, he is."

Grace winced. "I heard him yelling at you. Just think, you could have had an inside source on how to butter him up, but you decided you like surprises." Bending, she retrieved a flat of empty berry pints and her flashlight, finding his red eyes traveling up her body as she straightened, warming her with their garnet glow. "But I need to have a word with him about how we treat guests."

Merrick waved off her suggestion. "He wasn't so bad . . . stubborn, but not unwilling to hear me out, which is more than I can for the gryphon I met with earlier today. I *will* admit I've been remiss in my belief that centaurs were part horse, though. Mules. Stubborn, cranky mules. Who knew? You look beautiful, by the way." He drew forward slowly as he spoke, lightly smoothing a lock of hair behind her ear, making her shiver beneath his soft touch.

"Better not let him catch you saying that, stubborn mules have quite a kick."

The sounds of crickets and frogs receded in the wake of her thumping heartbeat, anticipating his lips meeting hers as he lowered his head slowly. Her face tilted up, her eyes slipped closed, *expectancy* weighting the air . . . Instead, his fangs nipped at her earlobe, and she was glad for the hand she still had on the table at her back. Tris was right, she decided. *Here for a good time, but not a long time. Make the most of it.* She still didn't like the way her heart quivered at the thought of him flying out of her life nearly as abruptly as he'd flown into it, but her heart had made mistakes before. Sleep with him, get it out of your system. Then you can decide whether or not you want to see him again. She was not enthused over her Tris's suggestion of a compiled list, but a short-term fuck buddy might be just what she was looking for.

"Well, let's not waste time talking about him, then. We have berries to find."

"It's not that I didn't like living in the city, but I don't think I could go back, at least not anytime soon. My parents are still there, but they live on opposite sides of town, and I didn't really have anyone I was close to anymore, not close enough to make me stay."

Grace bit her lip and glanced away, unsure if her words made her sound as pathetic as they made her feel. For someone who was self-admittedly awkward and antisocial, he had a way of asking questions that cut to the quick, bypassing all of her sunny defenses.

She hadn't moved away so much as she'd run away, but how could she admit that as a grown woman? That she picked up and left her life behind to start anew, that it had been easier to forge new friendships than to deal with the isolation she'd felt amongst those existing ones? People didn't talk about marital problems, at least her friend group hadn't. You either had a glossy, perfect, social media-ready life with well-coiffed children and beach vacations, or you were divorced. Ladies' night outings and online dating and *getting back out there*. There was no middle in either situation. No one admitted when there was trouble at home, or talked about separations, or arguments, or therapy. Newly divorced was only acceptable with a haircut and a new wardrobe and a zeal for finding a new true love, and Grace had possessed none of that. Running away from her life had been a relief, and she couldn't talk about that either.

Instead, she grinned up at the handsome mothman, leading him back to safer conversational waters. "So you said Cal was receptive to your suggestions? How many things will we need to do?"

"What about your ex-husband?" Merrick pressed on, undeterred. Grace pursed her lips and scrunched her nose, gazing up at him, earning a lopsided smile in return, his antennae twitching. "I'm being horribly nosy, aren't I?"

"I don't know if I'd say *horribly* nosy," she conceded, matching his grin. "I guess it's probably normal to ask, right?" Grace paused, considering what she ought to say, what would sound better than 'I ran away from home and filed for divorce through the mail.' *The truth. Just tell him the truth.* She didn't have anything to hide, nor did she owe him anything. The berry tray was supported a few feet away on one of the cannily designed little stands Caleia had created, the pint-sized containers already heaped with the dark, sweet fruit. It would be time to leave soon, time to move on to the evening's next activity, and Grace was committed to ensuring that he was not the only one absent of clothing. She was ready to break the seal on their brief acquaintance; wanted a return to the heat of those two nights when he was outside her window. And if he needed a little bit of conversation to get him there, she thought, she would do whatever she needed to help him get it up.

"I left to get away from my ex-husband. And he wasn't my ex yet when I left. I guess I really didn't do anything the right way, but it just seemed like the easiest way at the time. The best decision. And it was, really. I really do love the life I've built here, and if I had to go back and redo things, I don't think that I would choose to do it differently. I probably would have left earlier, that's it." Grace glanced up, taking in his furrowed brow and narrowed eyes. "It wasn't abusive, if that's what you're thinking," she said quickly. "At least, not physically. It just . . . wasn't healthy."

"Not healthy," he echoed. "I don't want to make you talk about painful things, but is there someone I need to drop off a bridge somewhere?"

"See, I *knew* you had a thing about bridges! 'Urban legend' my ass." His laughter was a low hum, a deep acoustic buzz she felt beneath her skin, a sensation she thought she could get used to. "You don't strike me as the violent type, you know."

"Oh, I'm not," he chuckled, tightening her stomach with its low vibration, the resonance of which went right between her thighs. "I'm a lover, not a fighter . . . " As he spoke, a berry was raised to her mouth, pressing enough to burst the juice across her lips in a wet smear before dragging it down her chin. " . . . but there are exceptions to every rule."

The berry finally found its way into her mouth as she grinned up, letting him admire his handiwork. "That's good, I don't care much for fighters."

"And your ex was a minotaur, right? There's a minotaur who works here, I saw him as we were heading out to the field."

"There is," she agreed, plucking a berry from the nearest bush and holding it up to his mouth, shivering when he grazed her fingertip with one of those fangs. Heat coiled through her at the wet, warm feel of his mouth and the sudden memory of that delicious, sucking pressure. When his long-fingered hand spread over her hip, she decided to try pushing her luck. "He's a good guy . . . he's been trying to fuck me for the past two years. Got pretty close a few weeks ago."

The hand at her hip tightened and his eyes flashed a darker red as he tugged her closer.

"Perfect. I hate everything about him." The next berry he lifted was one he'd already bitten, and the juice dribbled over her collarbone as the pulpy fruit was dragged down her neck. Grace's indignant laugh at the movement cut off on a gasp when something long and wet moved over the top of her breasts, exposed in the scant fabric of the sundress, before laving at the juice that pooled in the hollow of her throat. Merrick hadn't moved: still loomed over her, gripping her hip, his garnet eyes glittering in the moonlight.

The kiss they'd shared on the observatory balcony had been very nice — his small fangs had nipped at her lips and she'd gone dizzy over the warm, woodsy smell of him — but there'd been something missing, and now she knew why. His tongue was an impossibly long coil, leaving his mouth in an endless line, and he used it to lick at her skin, up her neck to the corner of her mouth, cleaning the trails of dark berry juice he'd smeared there. A rush of wetness joined the heat between her legs when she considered how dexterous this extra-long appendage might be.

"I thought you said you weren't a fighter?"

"I'm not, but I never said anything about not being the jealous type," he murmured once his tongue had re-coiled itself in his mouth. The desire to have his hands moving over her body, to strip off her dress and bare herself for that curious tongue nearly made her dizzy, bracing herself with a palm against his chest as he continued. "That's going to make it very hard to be nice to him. I'll do my best not to act like a jealous asshole every time I'm here, but no promises."

"And how often will that be?" Tracing her fingertip over his sharp clavicle, she managed to avoid his eye as she gave voice to the thoughts that had been running on a loop in her head since Tris's message. *Here for a good time, but not a long time.* "After all, you probably won't be sticking around for long, right? Once the birds and the bats start migrating you'll be on your way?" The berry she raised to his mouth was dark and ripe, the flesh bursting easily against the gleaming white fang to which she pressed it; the pulpy sweet juice a wet pressure against her lips when she moved the fruit back to her own mouth, dragging it back and forth.

Merrick's expression was inscrutable, but the hand he kept at her hip tightened infinitesimally as he clicked. "It depends how long the program lasts. That's usually out of my control." His voice was a mellifluous hum, raising the fine hair on her neck. His antennae fluttered low around his ears and her resolve wavered.

"Then I suppose we ought to make the most of it," she said lightly. The hand that suddenly gripped her wrist was strong, his movements so quick she had no time to react. The dripping berry at her lips was dragged down her neck and pressed to her throat, the pressure increasing as he slowly pulled it lower. She gasped when the macerated remains of the fruit slipped between her breasts, guided by his leading fingers, her nipples tightening beneath the thin cotton dress.

"I suppose you're right." The ability to breathe was not one she regularly contemplated, but at that moment, as his fingers pressed beneath the edge of her bra, his warm, berry-smeared palm cupping her breast, her lungs were completely unable to inflate in the wake of his softly spoken words.

When his head lowered, practically necessitating him bending in half, she was ready to receive the kiss. Heat and warmth, the intoxicating smell of him and the sharp, sweet taste of blackberries, the long fingers that rolled her nipple making her moan into his mouth. *This is all you're looking for. A good time*. Despite the desire there, his mouth was still somewhat hesitant and undemanding, making her feel as though she was completely in control of how the evening ended; control she valued more than he could possibly suspect.

"If you're planning on coming around to check up on us often, I'll see if we can have a designated parking spot for the lab coat know-it-all."

A gasp of mock offense accompanied the berry he smushed against her cheek, once again dragging it into her dress, ignoring her squeal of laughter. Catching the devious hand as it dropped the smashed fruit to the ground before he could snatch it away, her lips closed over the pad of his tapered thumb. Sucking the berry juice from his skin, her tongue slid over his knuckle, eliciting a purring growl from his fluff-covered throat.

"You're making it very difficult to be a gentleman." His thumb withdrew, running over her teeth, testing their sharpness before leaving her mouth. Before she could protest, two long fingers replaced it, sticky with berry pulp.

The thought of those same impossibly long fingers curling into her wet heat, pressing into that spot that made her back arch and toes curl pulled a moan from her throat, vibrating around his fingers in her mouth. Merrick's answering groan was accompanied by a bruising pressure at her hip, crushing her against him. If this was a test, Grace considered, she planned on passing it.

Stroking the underside of the slim digits with her tongue made his antennae shiver and dance, while hollowing her cheeks and sucking made his dusk-colored wings flutter wildly, as that impossible tongue unspooled from his mouth to drop into the loose fabric of her dress. The thin, wet slither over her breasts made her shiver; when it dropped even lower to slide over her stomach she gasped.

"You're right. I want to have another taste." His voice was deep and guttural, another buzz at her neck, his rapidly beating wings a fluttering buzz that seemed to surround her; that low hum emanated through her, buzzing against her hands splayed against his chest, buzzing against her neck where his fangs pressed into her lightly, buzzing against her clit when that impossible, miraculous tongue slid beneath her panties to drag through through her wet folds.

The confirmation that it had been his tongue he had used that night from the tree outside her window, unfurling and stretching from the branches made her weak. When the tip dragged back through her slick to alight on her clit, sucking with strength of a small vacuum, the noise that left her throat was loud enough to send a cluster of starlings zooming through the sky, startled from a nearby tree, her knees buckling, no longer willing to support her.

"Wait!"

His tongue retreated as he caught her, cradling her securely against him as she reeled.

"Wait . . . not here. Cal might come outside." As soon as the words were out, she caught the smell of woodsmoke carrying on the light breeze, which she'd attributed to Merrick's appealingly smokey smell when she'd been pressed to him.

"Do you want to come back to my place?" he asked serious-ly, the somberness of his tone making it sound as if he were asking her to come over so he could audit her taxes. "Do you want to come over for sex?"

His matter-of-factness was adorably hilarious, she decided, nearly choking on her laughter. Terribly literal, he was leaving nothing to chance this time.

"I know you have to do some work at home, right? Are you going into the lab?" she asked, thinking through the logistics of proximity to her house versus his own.

His head shook, feathery antennae dancing. "I'm not, ac-tually. Today was a fieldwork day. This is the fourth farm I've been to since this afternoon. But," he added with a frown, "I *do* still have to record my data at home."

"Perfect," she grinned. "I've always wanted to see an apart-ment in the woods." *Here for a good time, not a long time.* It was fine, she reminded herself. This was all she needed — scratch this itch, and then she could get back to business, without feeling as if there was something missing in her life. *Make the most of it.* "You can be a gentleman tomorrow morning when you make me breakfast. Let's go back to your place. For sex."

By the time she'd arrived at the edge of the dark forest, her berry patch bravado had withered and fled. Grace was reminded once more that she wasn't actually that brave, wasn't that bold, and away from the false sanctity of her bedroom, she was the furthest thing from brazen that one could imagine.

"You know the way?" Merrick had asked as he crouched next to her car window in the small gravel lot. She would drive herself, it was decided, since he had flown. The notion of a partner who was able to fly was dumbfounding, even here, even in Cambric Creek, and she'd decided she'd feel better driving this first night they were together.

She'd been giddy as she pulled out of the farm. She wondered if being with him would have the same raw excitement as performing for him had; if they would have any awkwardness, learning to maneuver together for the first time. She realized that those two nights in her bedroom, even though he had been right there outside the window, she'd felt buffered by the safety of her own home, secure in the knowledge that all she had to do was drop the shade. Here though, at his house, she would be at his mercy.

She was comfortable in her own skin in the privacy of her own four walls, never thought twice about her thick thighs as she sat on her sofa in the evenings, laptop open to her reliable, color-coded spreadsheets. She had the heart-stopping supposition that he might be disappointed in her body as she stopped for a red light, midway across town. It was one thing for him to have happened upon a naked woman gyrating in front of her open window, one thing to have stopped and enjoyed the titillating show. It was a wholly different scenario to have her back at his place, in his bed, where he would see her dimpled ass up close and personal, without the forgiving cover of branches masking her flaws. *Oh well*, she thought. *Like it or lump it, I guess.*

Arriving at the dark house, she swallowed down her trepidation. It's fine, Grace told herself. It's totally fine. She was hooking up for the first time in ages with a guy she genuinely liked, to whom she was extremely attracted; she was going to his house, she was alone in the dark, and it was going to be *just fine. This is why you shouldn't have stopped taking Prozac.*

The troll family — a professional couple and their eight rambunctious children — had lived in a grand house on a large wooded lot. She was familiar with the neighborhood, and Merrick had provided exacting directions before kissing her on the cheek, gathering himself up and launching straight up into the air, his giant wings catching easily. His instructions had been to pull past the house, following the driveway until she'd reached the large barn, and he'd be waiting for her there. The large red barn loomed ahead as she pulled up the long driveway, edging past the house until the concrete turned to gravel. Merrick was nowhere to be found, but as she stepped from the car, she was able to see dozens of flickering lights in the dark field beyond, a sight that was as spellbinding as it was unexpected. *Lanterns*, she realized. Suddenly Merrick was there, melting out of the darkness like a tall shadow, smiling as she stepped from the car.

He'd lined a path through the darkness for her, the flickering lanterns giving the journey across the long meadow a storybook feel as she gripped his strong arm, holding her basket of berries tightly in the crook of the other, unsure of where she was being led. Fireflies flickered and danced, bobbing between the lanterns as she passed, crickets chirped, and she could hear the occasional flutter of wings, either bats or starlings, swooping overhead. It was magical. She'd witnessed moments like this before, on the farm — long after the workers had left for the day and the livestock secured in their pens. Caleia's ancient tree would be lit with fairy lights, the sound of tree frogs and cicadas and the lone, melancholy strains of a violin coming from Callum's small cottage splitting the night, making her feel a million miles away from the city, despite being just outside it.

Merrick had wrapped his spindly fingers securely over the hand she'd circled around his forearm, leading her through the glimmering darkness with careful, confident steps. Gliding through the lantern-lit field with him was like something out of a fairytale, and in those brief moments she forgot her nerves, forgot the invisibility she'd felt for the past decade, forgot that she'd been out of the game for what felt like an eternity. There was nothing in the world but her, the tall moth at her side, and this beautiful field of flickering gold. *He's sweet and funny and he made this magical field of light just for you.*

The trail of lanterns ended as the forest abruptly rose up at the edge of the meadow, black and ominous and full of whispers, and Grace remembered that fairy tales often had dark twists and turns. The tall trees blocked out the light of the bright moon, and the flickering lanterns at her back cast jumping shadows at her feet, adding to the rising panic that suddenly suffused her without welcome. Anxiety had always been a tricksy squatter in her life, often letting her think it had gone for good, just before popping out to ruin a good mood, as it did then.

Her feet had turned to lead at the treeline, leaving her slightly breathless, gulping down her nerves. There had been a short-tempered boggart who lived in the woods behind her grandparent's house when she was a child. There had been an incident with the creature involving her older brother when she was just a baby, and while she never knew the specifics, she'd heard whispers of the Otherworld over the years, and she'd never been allowed to play there unsupervised, her head filled with stories of the dangers that lurked in the trees, particularly after dark. The woods beyond her now were black as pitch, and the soft sounds of the open field seemed distant as she strained to listen for the snapping of twigs that might indicate something lurking ahead.

Merrick's wings fluttered as she jerked to a stop, looking down in concern, his long antennae twitching. "It-it's only a little ways in," he stammered, loosening his grip on her arm, to her dismay. His forehead bunched at her obvious panic, antennae flattening out against his head. "I-I don't want you to be uncomfortable or a-afraid . . . this was a bad idea. I'm so sorry . . . let me walk you back to your car at least." The confidence he'd had in the dark berry patch shriveled in the face of her hesitation, the nervous stammer and twitchiness he'd displayed the very first night he'd sought her out at the farm returning, his shoulders hunching and wings fluttering anxiously. When he gingerly took her arm again, it was with the very tips of his fingers, his body angled away from hers.

The entire evening — soft and perfect and lovely as it had been—came crashing down around her as he clicked in distress, turning to lead her back through the romantic field he'd prepared so that she'd be able to see her way through the darkness.

"Wait!"

His jaw clenched, his antennae remained low against his head, and the way he held himself carefully away from her was enough to snap her out of the momentary panic. Wrapping her hand around his, she looked up imploringly, but his red eyes were resolutely fixed above her head, away from hers for the first time that night. "Wait, I-I don't want to leave. I just—"

"It's fine, Grace. You don't need to do anything you're not comfortable with," he interrupted gently. "I-I don't want you to be afraid...of me."

Her head whipped up at his words. *He thinks you're afraid of him?!* "No! That's not it at all! I-I'm not afraid of you, of course I'm not afraid of you!"

"The humans I've worked with—"

"I'm nothing like the humans you've worked with," she cut him off. "And I told you before, you don't have to worry about that anymore. Or at least as long as you're here. You're probably not even the only mothman on this block, did you know that? You need to start socializing." Questioning red eyes met hers at last, and she took the opportunity to thread her fingers with his, squeezing lightly. "It's the woods . . . I've always been afraid of the woods."

"The woods?" he echoed with a cock of his head, glancing to the dark trees. "It-it's only a little ways . . . you don't need to go into the woods, it's fine. Let me walk you back to—"

"No!" Now both hands wrapped around his arm, and she found herself tugging him forward, towards the black forest. "I don't want to go home . . . unless you want me to leave." The thought brought heat to her cheeks, but he quickly shook his head, antennae bobbing.

"No, of course not. It-it really is just a little ways in." He stared at her hands wrapped around his arm as he spoke, his wings twitching. "I wouldn't let anything happen to you."

His voice was low, a deep vibration that she felt buzz up her back and she shivered, stepping a bit closer to his warmth. "Well, lead the way. Just don't let go of my hand."

True to his word, the large tree was less than twenty feet into the dark forest and she remained unmolested, Merrick's strong arm beneath hers and a guiding hand at her back, ensuring she didn't stumble or fall. There was a circular staircase wrapping up the base of the tree and a glance upwards showed a long climb into the dark branches above.

"This is going to be a lot faster if you let me . . ." Grace didn't balk when he scooped her up, bridal style.

She expected to be assaulted with branches as he shot into the air, but within a matter of what seemed like seconds, they'd arrived at the circular platform he called home, and she realized just how high up they were. Walking to the railing once her knees had stopped shaking, she couldn't suppress a gasp as she looked out over the edge. The view was spectacular.

The entire forest was laid out before her, and the valley beyond. The open fields of farmland, the winking lights of the Cambric Creek — they were all visible as she stood breathless at the top of the world.

"It's a great view," he murmured unnecessarily, the heat of him close at her back. He stepped away quickly when she turned, relieving her of the basket and throwing his arm open. "Make yourself at home."

The entire space was one giant room, the only walls belonging to two partitioned areas that hugged the trunk, a bathroom and perhaps a laundry facility, she assumed. A thick tube of cables ran up the tree, humming with energy, and realized that it must have been the electric and plumbing lines. A retractable roof and screened surround kept the treetop dwelling protected from the elements, he explained.

"They spent an obscene amount of money on this thing, but the rent's not terrible," Merrick laughed, crossing the expansive space. There was a work table, cluttered with papers and books and several large tanks, which he leaned over. There was flitting movement in one of the tanks, and as she moved to stand at his side, she saw what she thought must be bumblebees.

"Hummingbirds," he corrected. "Black-throated mangoes. They're native to South America. I spent three semesters there a few years ago, and one of my colleagues in that lab sent me the eggs after their nests were destroyed in a storm. We don't know what happened to their mothers. I incubated these four, but their circadian rhythm orgainzation is all over the place, which is what I'm studying . . . you're supposed to be asleep," he scolded the tiny birds, and she had to reach out to steady herself on the table, lest she melt into a puddle of smitten goo as he fed the birds with a tiny dropper, scratching each one gently on the neck before turning away to jot something in a notebook next to their enclosure.

"Maybe they're just following along with what they see their new momma doing," she laughed, remembering the story he'd told her about the bats he'd weaned.

He smiled as he wrote, giving her a flash of those small fangs again before clicking in disapproval at the buzzing little balls of feathers. "Well, that's a working theory. They're contrary little brats, that's another."

The heat she felt curl through her core reminded her why she was there — she was going to learn what his weight felt like above her, how soft his velvety skin would be against every part of her. "So, your prior experiences with your co-workers . . . does this mean you've never dated a human before?" *Never **been** with a human . . .*

"No, I haven't." His voice was low as he clicked and shook out his mantle, avoiding her eye. "I hope I'm not doing everything wrong."

The air outside was balmy and warm, despite the slight breeze at the top of the tree, a perfect summer night, as she settled against the cushions of the upholstered chaise lounge, patting the spot beside her as he chirped nervously once more.

"I had a great time at the observatory, and tonight has been wonderful so far, so I think you're doing okay."

"Ah," he began in a low rumble that made her toes curl, settling beside her, "but the night is young." His wide hand spread out over the side of her hip as his head lowered and Grace felt her heart climb into her throat in excitement over the kiss she knew was coming. "There's plenty of time for me to screw something up."

Buzzing. That was all she was capable of focusing on as Merrick's mouth moved on her own before trailing hungrily to her ear. The thrumming vibration of his wings, moving rapidly as his lips hummed at her throat, the feathery brush of his antennae caressing her face, his long fingers fisting in her dress . . . and the buzzing, guttural groan that seemed to erupt from his throat as her legs fell open for him.

"That *smell* . . . you smell incredible. How are you able to smell so good?" he groaned, his deep voice was a muffled slur against her skin, kissing across her collarbone, tongue dropping from his mouth once more.

He'd talked about how good she smelled once before, Grace realized, the night he'd apologized for watching her from the tree. *Much sweeter than the berries.* Merrick's thin, almost lipless mouth trailed down her neck and over her chest, his long fingers fisted in her dress, which he'd bunched at her hips. The realization that it was the smell of her arousal he was enamored with hit her just as that long tongue curled over the dampened front of her panties, pulling a strangled moan from her.

"I need to taste you . . . "

The mattress of the big platform bed to which he carried her was springy and soft, around the tree trunk from where they'd been sitting. The circular platform of his rented home had spectacular views from every side, but the area where the bed resided looked out over the valley, unobstructed. Grace sat up on her knees as he gripped the bottom hem of her short dress, pulling it up over her thick thighs and round ass, catching on the shelf of her breasts before tugging over her head. She unclasped her bra with one hand as he tossed the dress aside, noting his shuddering breath as he took her in.

"You've never been with a human before?" she questioned again, eyebrow raised. He was practically hovering off the ground in anxious desire, chest heaving, antennae dancing wildly.

"Never," he wheezed.

She straightened up as he approached the bed, pushing her chest out a bit when she noticed that his hands were twitching, fighting the instinct to reach out and touch her. Leading his wrists, she guided him to cup one creamy globe and then the other, releasing her grip as he tested their weight, the silky velvet pad of his thumbs gently circling over puckered pink buds.

"Are you sure you're not one of those mothmen who like to play bedroom bingo with human women?" He sputtered at the question, flailing in place, and she laughed, closing her fingers over his hands to keep him in place until he kneaded her flesh once more. He too had lost his berry-patch bravery, it seemed, and the thought brought a flush to her neck. There was an odd responsibility in being his first human, the first of her species he would taste and touch, the first human who would touch and taste him in return. *We're going to need to make this an experience he remembers.*

The thought of being the first human to suckle on his cock tip was exhilarating, the flush spreading down her chest. Gripping one of his wrists again, she led his hand down her body, over the soft swell of her stomach, curling his fingers over her plump mound, pressing their velvety softness into her slippery, slick heat. Her eyes slipped shut as the sound filled the room, the same high-frequency buzzing that had enveloped her as she knelt on her bed in front of the window. Grace couldn't tell if the sound originated from his chest or from his wings, or some other unfamiliar bit of his anatomy she was unable to identify, but as her eyes slipped shut, she felt as if she were once again outlined in the golden glow of her bedroom light, kneeling in front of the window for his unseen audience on the other side.

She dragged a finger through her hot folds, spreading open the lips of her sex until she reached her ravenous, dripping cunt. Sliding a finger into herself with a breathy sigh, her hips pushed until she had reached the top knuckles. The sensation of her long curls brushing against the middle of her back as she rolled her neck made her shiver, pushing out her chest for him again, pulling the finger back until she was able to add a second, sliding them back in. For a moment, that was good enough. She rocked against the two fingers within her, using her wrist to direct their pumping motion, squeezing her inner muscles around them. It felt good, *so* good. She bit her lip as she whimpered, breasts bouncing as she finger fucked herself for her audience, using the springiness of the mattress for her momentum as she rocked.

When she managed to find that spot within her that made her toes curl, she moaned. *So good.* Merrick grunted in response, the buzzing around her increasing. His reaction made her cry out again, improving the show. After all, Grace thought, she wanted her audience to enjoy an immersive experience.

"It feels so good," she moaned, increasing the force she used to bounce against the fingers, fucking herself deeply on their length. She wanted to ride his cock this way, and hoped she'd get the chance that night. Her breath had begun to come out in short pants, timed to the solid thrust of the fingers, keening as they rubbed over her G-spot repeatedly. She wanted to come for him like this, wanted to let him see the flush on her tits and the way her head dropped back as her body clenched, closer and closer to her peak with every roll of her hips. She needed more, though. She needed pressure on her clit, moving some in place to roll over, crying out when it hit just the right spot.

"I want to come for you," she keened. "Do you want to feel me come?" His answering moan came out on a hiss, unable to form words, telling her all she needed to know about his enjoyment of the events thus far.

After that, she was in a race against herself, increasing the speed of her hips, thrusting herself against the fingers instead of moving them against her. The thumb rolled over her clit, the long fingers within her dragging against her G-spot, until her thighs began to quiver. She'd never been a squirter before, but she was certain she would be able to chase the sensation in this position, if only she weren't so desperate to come. When the first wave of her orgasm quivered up her back, she was left breathless and gasping, unable to even cry out as her body seized, cunt clenching. She squeezed tight around the two fingers inside of her, her mouth open in a silent moan as she came, clutching convulsions throbbing through her.

When the sensation of shaking apart finally ebbed away, she moaned at last, withdrawing the fingers from her body. Their velvet was stained dark, coated in her slick, his chest heaving as he pulled his hand out of her grip, pushing the fingers that had been inside of her through his lips, sucking them clean with a groan. She enjoyed masturbating for him, it was as simple as that, she thought shakily. And from what she could tell by the bulge in his smooth groin, he had enjoyed it as well. Something had been excited there, just inside his skin, and Grace wanted to tease it out, wanted to tease it and taste it with her tongue, wanted to learn if it would feel as good inside her as his fingers had.

He didn't give her the chance. She found herself pushed back to the mattress, her head reeling as she stared up at the tree platform's high ceiling, her thighs pushed open before he settled his shoulders between them.

"I want to taste you," he groaned, "*really* taste you. I want to drink right from your pussy. Can I?"

She nodded, closing her eyes again as his mouth lowered, his lips meeting her lips in a slow, sensual kiss, his aquiline nose pushing between them, opening her up for his hungry mouth. Grace once more felt enveloped in that buzzing hum as he groaned against her heat, drinking up her juices like he wanted to drown in her. He began to hum as his mouth neared the heat of her slick, pink center. Grace was engulfed in fire as he groaned in unrestrained pleasure, having reached his destination at last, sinking his tongue into her greedily.

She would never again be eaten out this well or enthusiastically, she realized. *Note to self: mothmen love eating pussy.* His long nose bumped her clit as he slipped and sucked on the slippery evidence of her orgasm, groaning his pleasure in a way that sent vibrations ricocheting up her spine, making her thighs tremble anew.

The long taper of his tongue pressed through her folds, buzzing and curling around her clit and almost causing her to become airborne again as she arched off the bed before it dipped lower, seeking the source of the smell that had his antennae dancing madly over her exposed skin. When his tongue dipped into her, Merrick's moan reverberated through her core, shaking through her body.

The endless length was a slithering, probing, cock-like intrusion that had her fisting the bedding as he pressed into her walls, finding the spot inside her that made her see stars. She had never had her G-spot *licked* before, but now that she had, nothing else would ever suffice again. There was no toy, no vibrator or dildo that could ever match the sensation of his long, unspooled tongue laving over the spot like a serpent, making her legs kick and thrash, as if she were having some sort of fit. There would be no matching this sensation, Grace thought, nothing he could possibly do to top this. The thick, silky pile of his ruff tickled against the inside of her thighs, and the smooth velvet of his fingertips rubbed against the back of her knees, where he spread her legs open, to better access his feast. Nothing would compare to this, at least that's what she thought.

But then his tongue receded, slurping its way free, before it moved to curl around her clit once more. The tapered tip curled and stroked, slipping an edge under the pearl's sensitive hood, an action that simultaneously liquefied her bones and tensed every muscle in her body. Around and around, it polished the slippery-slick surface of her engorged bud, leaving her a trembling wreck, barely able to cry out, until the tip of his tongue fastened over it, fastened over it with a hollowed end, and began to suck.

Grace was concerned for a moment that she had paralyzed herself. So violently did she arch off the mattress when he began to suck her, that she was unable to feel her legs for several quivering, star-seeing moments. *This* was what he had done to her that night, she realized. His endless coil of a tongue had reached right into her room, right to where she knelt at the foot of her bed before the window, sucking on her clit until she had almost passed out — and now she was going to pass out again. Consciousness seemed a thready, inconsistent thing, and her vision was alternating between black spots and bright white light that made her squint against its brilliance, her very soul threatening to leave her body, sucked through her clit by this voyeuristic, vacuum-tongued fiend. There was no better way to lose it, she decided.

"I-I'm going to come. Sweet merciful *fuck*, I'm going to come." His response to her warning was a click and chirp, a sound of delight, and she realized that was exactly what he wanted. Her second orgasm of the night was a shaking wave that rippled down to her toes as he worked her clit unceasingly, a sustained sensation that left her twitching helplessly.

She realized that was his plan as he continued sucking and licking and groaning against her, unable to get enough of the wetness that now glistened from his nose and chin, making her toes curl and legs shake until she begged him to stop, too oversensitized for the onslaught to continue. His chirp of disappointment had her shoulders shaking in laughter she was unable to contain as he crawled up her body. *Pussy obsessed.* The ability to speak didn't return for several long minutes, as her body continued to quiver and pulse, thoroughly exhausted by his dedication.

"Well," she wheezed eventually, as he gently played with the ends of her hair, "I don't have words to describe how good that was." Grace laughed weakly as he clicked in satisfaction. "Are you sure you've never been with a human? Because there are human men out there who can't even *find* the clit, and here you are with a suction-powered homing device. It's almost not fair." He chirped again and she laughed, cuddling into the thick mantle of fluff, exactly the way she had in her daydreams.

He sighed contentedly, curling around her. "Can we do that again?"

"Merrick! I'm pretty sure you Hoovered an entire layer of nerve endings *off my clit. Obviously* we're going to do that again." Grace pushed herself up from the mattress, even though she could've easily cuddled against him and gone to sleep for a century. She had mothmen to take care of, cocks to tease out, first time with a human blow jobs to give. She was generously going to let him eat her pussy again, but not until she learned what kind of noises he made when he came. "But not until we take care of you first."

The corded muscle in the arms she gripped bunched, his mouth at her neck faltering, being replaced by a small, hesitant-sounding chirp. When she glanced down, it was to find the fluffy antennae which had been caressing her cheeks now flattened around his head.

"What's wrong?"

His brow furrowed as he clicked, saying nothing for a long, weighted moment before kissing her throat gently."You-y ou're so soft," he murmured, his voice a low hum. "So soft and delicate. I-I don't want to hurt you . . . " He remained unmoved when she laughingly assured him she wouldn't break. "Humans are fragile. I'm a lot stronger than I look."

Grace sighed, sitting back to look him over with a considering eye. Tormand had done a number on her head, that was what she'd told him. When she'd run away from her marriage, her self-confidence had already fallen through a layer of barely there thin ice, leaving her gasping and frozen in the clutches of anxiety and self-doubt. That had been three years ago, and she still sometimes woke up in the middle of the night, clenching against phantom insults and small little cuts that, when put together, resulted in a gaping gash of a wound.

The humans he'd worked with over the years, she realized, had done the same. Nervous uncertainty and social anxiety very well may have been his default state, but he seemed incredibly preoccupied with what humans thought and how he expected them to act, and she knew those assumptions were born out of experience. It didn't matter how much she told him that Cambric Creek was different. He would need to experience it for himself. He needed to get out, see the town, make some friends. *Here for a good time, not a long time.* She pursed her lips, pushing away her inner voice. He might leave when the semester was over, funding for his program slashed or a more enticing position appearing in some South American jungle . . . But maybe the next position, the next town or mountain or jungle lab wouldn't be as stress inducing, once he experienced Cambric Creek. *You're going to be his tour guide,* she decided. *But first, you're going to suck his cock.*

"You won't hurt me. And if you do something I don't like, I'll tell you, okay? And if you're not sure about something, just ask, and I'll do the same. This is the first time for both of us."

Garnet eyes avoided hers as she ran a hand down the long expanse of his body, his groin as soft and smooth as he was everywhere else. "There *is* something in here, right?" His nod was accompanied by a nervous laugh; a laugh that cut off on a gasp when she traced over the nearly-hidden slit in his skin. "Well, I would like to personally extend him an invitation to come out and play."

"Once it's out there's no—" His words choked off on a groan as she pressed lightly, encouraging his cock to unsheath. "Once it's out it's out."

"I get it, no takesies backsies once it's out . . . I don't intend on leaving you unsatisfied, you know."

A gust of wind suddenly shook the branches around them, loosing a spray of leaves into the loft, and Merrick took advantage of the distraction to vault himself from the bed, crossing to the trunk to hit the button that would extend the screen around the treetop dwelling. *He's not getting away that easily* . . . There was a thick sheepskin rug beside the bed, cushioning her knees as she dropped to the ground before him as he returned to her.

"You're not going to hurt me, and we're both going to have fun . . . okay?" His hip bones were sharp beneath her lips, but the velvet of his dusky grey skin was soft as ever as she kissed the concave hollow of his stomach. Above her, his breath came out on a ragged exhale, capitulating to her demands. She wondered if he could feel her smile against his skin as she kissed across his hips, listening to the soft chirps and clicks he made, paying attention for any note of distress.

The suppleness of his velvet dragged across her lips as she considered his trepidation. He was strong, yes, but that hadn't prevented any of the things he'd been only too happy to do with her up until that point. *Maybe he's worried about not satisfying you.* She didn't know anything about mothman anatomy, after all, maybe they were used to a speedy mating ritual . . . *his cock might be as long and thin as his tongue.* Still, she rationalized, he certainly knew how to use that tongue. *It doesn't matter.* She liked him, and she would figure out a way to make it work. She didn't know much about mothmen at all, she realized sheepishly. *Every day you need to learn something new, starting today. Every day until he leaves.*

The desperate chirps emitting from his throat had coalesced into something that resembled a buzzing whine as her mouth trailed lower, his long fingers winding into her hair to seek purchase against her scalp. When her lips landed at the top of the long slit in his velutinous skin, she felt a deep groan ripple down his spine; when she licked a wide stripe up the length of it, the hand at her head crushed her to his pelvis.

"I'm sorry!" he gasped, easing his grip, allowing her to pull back slightly.

There was a certain level of responsibility that came with being his first human, she thought again. He'd already seen to her pleasure, in the process of satisfying his own desperate desire to taste her, had expressed his nerves over her delicate anatomy and his fear of hurting her . . . he was doing everything right, and now she had a responsibility to ensure he enjoyed himself as much as she was. Running her palms down his long, leanly muscled thighs, she trailed a line of kisses up the length of his slit, following with her tongue once more. He was hot here, his skin heated by an internal fire bubbling beneath the surface of this intriguing opening, which had bulged beneath her mouth. The hands in her hair had returned with a lighter grip, although every pass of her tongue still earned a buzzing groan that seemed to vibrate in her core.

Grace used the tip of her index finger to stroke against the now slippery slit in his skin. She pressed into the opening, testing the give, finding that her finger was able to slip in easily. Hot and wet, slippery with a viscous lubrication, she stroked up the inside of the solid wall of muscle, feeling him quiver beneath her.

"Are you sensitive here?" She asked teasingly, clearly able to tell that he was, giggling at his slack-jawed nod."Is-is that okay?"

Merrick's fluffy antennae were standing on end, the long coil of his talented tongue hanging several inches out of his mouth. She could barely see his face around his puffed up mantle, but she managed to catch his wordless nod, that low hum the only sound he seemed capable of in the moment. Swirling her fingers, she coated them in his slippery lubrication before removing her hand to lick tentatively at her fingers. Salty and a bit sweet, not at all unpleasant. Grace grinned up at him, knowing exactly what she would do next.

When the hands at her head gently urged her forward, she resumed her attention on his slit. When her tongue pressed into the hot opening, it met the resistance of his cock, unseating slowly. The tip was smooth against her tongue, hot and wet, edging forward into the equally hot cavern of her mouth, and when she sucked it lightly, Merrick moaned, arching against her.

Dark pink and shiny, slick with its own lubrication, the tip tapered to an angled point and she tongued the flat edge of it. Her lips puckered around the slim length easily, she realized, not allowing herself to feel disappointed. *It'll just be different, that's all.* After all, she was having fun. *Besides, you've already seen what he can do with that tongue . . .* The slithering, slippery appendage had begun to widen at its base, and once the length in her mouth was equal to what one of his long fingers had felt like, she began to suck in earnest, gripping his trembling thighs for leverage. It might not be much, but that didn't mean she wasn't going to blow him like a pornstar.

She realized almost immediately her folly.

He surged forward, filling her mouth until she gagged, so wide that her jaw popped and it was a struggle to take a breath, until she pulled back gasping. It was shiny and wet, and what she'd assumed was the base was merely the start of the first swell. Slippery smooth and riddled with thick, pulsing veins, the vaguely S-shaped tentacle-like appendage was nothing she could have imagined.

Merrick's red eyes had widened in concern, the hand in her hair disentangling quickly.

"This is okay!" she quickly clarified, wrapping her hand around the thick bottom swell, as big as her fist. "This is . . . good. Very good."

Putting her mouth back to work, Grace resumed sucking on what she could comfortably fit in her mouth, using her hands to stroke the rest of the thick length, hoping he was reassured by her actions. His fingers re-tangled themselves in her hair, exerting the lightest pressure as she hummed, mimicking the steady, low sound he emitted. When his hips began to move, meeting her mouth, she released him with a wet *pop*, getting a good look at his fully unsheathed length. Thick and curving with a quivering tapered tip, his cock was more than she'd bargained for, and a ripple of concern for her cervical integrity moved up her back. *No takesies backsies . . .*

"C'mon big boy. I want to feel this monster inside me." Her voice displayed a bravado her lady garden didn't quite share, but 'fake it til you make it' had become her life's motto and she wasn't about to stop now. He was fully erect and, if his lightly thrusting hips were any indication, ready to fuck her into the next day, and she was going to make sure he enjoyed himelf as much as she'd enjoyed his oral ministrations, she decided, squaring her shoulders. She found herself being lifted back to the bed easily, legs spread wide as Merrick vibrated above her. The soft, wet glide of his tongue against her clit had her gasping in pleasure once more, before she felt the press of that tapered tip. He rocked gently, teasing her with the first several inches of his cock, his long fingers rubbing circles against her until she thought she'd go mad from the teasing sensation.

"M-more . . . please, more." The thick bottom swell of his curving cock was a heavy pressure, and her eyes teared as it pushed into her, stretching far past the point of comfort.

"Is-is this okay?" he asked through clenched teeth, his control growing thin now that he was seated within her clenching heat.

"It's okay," she gasped, breathing around the stab of pain. "Ju-just give me a second to adjust . . . " Merrick groaned as she shifted, lowering himself to lie above her, and a bolt of white pleasure wiped her vision as the top curve of his cock pressed into her. In this new, adjusted position she was able to feel every inch of him, and when he gave a shallow, tentative thrust, she cried out in pleasure. "Oh Gods, more! Just like that . . . more!"

He began rutting against her, that familiar low buzz settling around them, his cock thick enough to rub every inch of her, and she decided she was going to enjoy learning about mothmen, if he fucked her this way with any regularity.

Time ceased to exist as they fell into a dizzying, pleasurable pattern: he fucked her tirelessly, as the curling, slithering coil of his long tongue would unspool between their bodies to lick and suck on her clit, bringing her to a spine-rattling orgasm, when he would pull out and feast on the nectar of her cunt like he was guzzling down a chalice of ambrosia, stolen from the gods. His undulating cock would slide back into her and her eyes would practically roll out of her skull on every press of that thick swell, and he would begin the cycle over again until she was a shuddering, gasping mess.

She was positive the sky overhead was beginning to lighten when he began to vibrate. She was on her stomach at that point, as he hammered into her from behind. She felt the familiar buzzing of his wings and the vibration of his velvety smooth chest against her back, but that time it was different. His hips had taken on erratic rhythm, his arms jerking, even as he held her tightly, and for a moment, Grace was certain she was nearly able to feel the buzzing vibration within her.

Her legs were hooked over the awkward back joints of his insectoid lower legs, flush beneath him, and she nearly didn't notice when the mattress disappeared. They were several feet in the air, his great wings beating with his steadiness his hips no longer possessed, and without the bed buffering the vibrating sensation, she was able to tell that her initial suppositions were correct — his cock was vibrating inside her, along with something in his chest and the buzz of his wings, her teeth nearly rattling from the percussive force. When the tip of that sucking tongue once more closed over the swollen, aching clit, Grace thought she might shake apart right alongside him.

"I-I I'm about to finish, I can't hold it in. Do you want me to —"

"Finish inside me," she wheezed, her eyes crossing as he vibrated against her G-spot. If this was what all mothmen could do, someone needed to alert the media, alert congress! This needed to be the headline of every newspaper, the only story talked about on the news. *Hot single mothmen with Dyson-strength tongues and vibrating dicks are in a neighborhood near you!* Her words were all the permission he needed. Merrick let out a long, guttural groan, coming with a hot gush. Those small, gleaming fangs sank into the juncture of her neck and shoulder as he emptied himself into her, not quite hard enough to break the surface, but the flash of pain made her arch, squeezing around his cock, milking him through his endless orgasm, until the world went black and she was limp in his arms.

The world did not stay black for long. She didn't want to think about what sort of UTI she might get from the endless fucking she received, sliding off the edge of the bed on knees that only wobbled a little, she was relieved to note. Beside her, Merrick looked dead. She could see the slight rise and fall of his fluffy mantle, assuring her that he'd not expired as he ejaculated, but he did not stir as she tiptoed off in search of the bathroom. When she returned, however, he was sitting on the edge of the bed, rubbing a hand over his eyes.

"Did-did you want me to bring you home, or —"

"I guess that depends on whether you're kicking me out or not?"

He sat up in panic, mouth dropping open. "N-no no, you don't have to leave. You never have to leave! I-I mean — I mean you're more than welcome to stay the night." She raised an eyebrow when he pulled himself up from the bed, motioning for her to claim it. "I don't actually sleep here, at least not very often."

There was a chair just around the bend from the bed, with a cannily designed open back. Beside it sat a small table housing a book, a notepad, and coffee cup. Grace smiled softly, evidence of his daily life that made her stomach flip-flop. He was soft and sweet, and it didn't matter if he wasn't going to be around for long. She liked him, and she wanted to be someone he would remember fondly. His wings slipped through the back of the chair, and when she climbed into his lap, cuddling against the thick mound of fluff — so like her daydreams, that Grace wasn't sure where her fantasies ended and reality began.

"You haven't seen much of downtown yet, right?" When he shook his head, she smiled again, rubbing his chest. "Okay, good. Every week we're going to go someplace different. By the end of summer, you'll have seen the whole town." She was going to learn something new about mothpeople at least every week, if not every day, she vowed. She was going to show him around and they were going to have fun together, for as long as it lasted. *Here for a good time, not a long time. Day one*, Grace thought, her eyes closing, the weight of his fingers in her hair pushing her down. *Vibrating cocks. That's definitely something new.*

CHAPTER SEVEN

Seven

The morning was hazy and golden, the sky an unbroken expanse of blue, dotted here and there with puffy white clouds, mirroring the sheep in the east pasture. The grass in the fields would still be coated in a cold sheen of dew, much like the long expanse of green she'd walked barefoot through earlier that morning, carrying her sandals and leaning on a strong, velvety arm. The sky had been a watercolor wash of pinky-gold then, the sun only just beginning to peak over the tops of the tall trees. She couldn't help but smile at the memory as her little car passed the corn, wavering in the breeze. It had been a beautiful morning. *A perfect start to the day, after a perfect night.*

As the car bumped along, the bucolic setting was marred by something looming in the distance. Grace frowned. A dark shape in the center of the gravel drive, standing before the closed wooden gate. She had left for work early, it was true, but surely the gates should be open by now? The employees who tended the animals, who worked in the fields, they would have arrived hours earlier, and Caleia always made sure to have the gate open for . . . *oh for fuck's sake.*

Caleia.

There had been a string of text messages, each one more exclamatory than the last, delivered the previous night, which she'd read for the first time that morning.

Hey, do you want to grab pizza?

I'm craving that greasy dump by the college

I'll be over in a bit

As the car grew closer to the gate, the shape coalesced into the figure of the graceful dryad, standing sentinel in the road, preventing Grace from entering. She grit her teeth, not wanting to deal with her friend's hysteria first thing in the morning.

I'm sitting in your driveway, but the house is dark and your car is gone

I'm assuming you're not home?

You really need to leave a lamp on or something, btw

Wait, were you going out with that guy again tonight?

I thought that wasn't until the weekend!

Please tell me you remembered cute underwear

Don't forget to call me when you get home! I want to hear everything!

Hello? Are you still alive? You better not have fallen asleep without calling me!

OMG

OMFG

YOU'RE FUCKING HIM AREN'T YOU

CALL ME!!!!!

Caleia stood in the center of the road scowling, arms thrown open to symbolically block the way, as if the wooden gate wasn't doing the job on its own. Grace slowed to a stop with a glower of her own. *Here we go...*

"Well, look what the wampus dragged in," the little nymph sneered, holding fast to the gate. "Do you have any idea how worried I was about you? I cannot *believe* you went on your first second date in a hundred years and didn't immediately call your best friend the *instant* you got home. I stayed up all night waiting!"

Grace leaned out the car window, mirroring Caleia's wrinkled nose. She'd texted her friend just before sunrise, reminding the nymph that she'd see her at work soon, and would bring her up to speed then. Apparently that answer had not sufficed.

What she *hadn't* mentioned was that when she'd sent the text there had been a firm, downy chest beneath her cheek that she'd been nuzzling into. His ergonomic moth chair had been surprisingly comfortable, and she'd fallen asleep against him, beneath the wide-open canopy of stars at the top of his tree. When she'd woken, the sky was a pink-tinged violet, a white-gold glow just beginning to lighten the world at the edge of the treeline. She'd been buffered from the dawn's chill by his velvet-covered wings, tenderly folded around her, and it had been impossibly comfortable there in his arms.

"Um, I texted you this morning, which you didn't bother responding to. Will you please open the gate? I have a wedding consultation this morning, and you know how mothers of the bride can be."

"I don't care that you texted this morning!" Caleia shot back defiantly, her long, chocolate brown waves glinting in the sun. "I wanted to talk to you as soon as you—" She broke off on a gasp, outrage forgotten. "Holy shit, you *did* fuck him! In! Right now! I want to hear all the gory details!"

Grace steeled herself, settling back against her seat with a sigh as Caleia activated the mechanism that swung the gate open. Years in wedding planning had taught her to be prepared for every scenario, which is why she always had a spare change of clothes in the trunk of her car, sparing her the indignity of having to do a walk of shame that morning — or worse, going to work wearing yesterday's dress. There really *was* a wedding consultation that morning, and at least now she could start her day.

Approximately an hour later, as she sat across the table from a pinched-face kitsune and her clearly overbearing mother, she realized she'd experienced a terrible lapse in judgment.

She'd expected that her first time back in the saddle after such a long drought would be a bumpy ride. She *hadn't* counted on being *in* said saddle for hours, the stamina of her slender, winged partner far greater than anything she was used to. Granted, Grace admitted, she'd gasped and moaned and writhed in pleasure the entire time they'd spent in his bed. His rutting hips had seemed indefatigable, his cock unable to be satisfied . . . and now she was paying the price for the enthusiastic all-night ride as she shifted on the unyielding bench of her gingham-covered picnic table.

She had never attempted to ride a unicycle down a mountain before, but she assumed that the achiness she felt that morning — bruised hips, sore thighs, and a sharp lance of pain shooting up her core every time she shifted her pelvis — had to be akin to the injuries one might acquire during such an excursion, and realized she most definitely should have called off. The hard bench was agony as the bride and her mother exchanged tense words over the guest list, and she wondered if she could have someone deliver one of those little doughnut-shaped hemorrhoid pillows from the pharmacy.

"If you don't want to have a big reception, you just need to say so. I don't mind being the bad guy here, I can call her this afternoon and let her know she needs to cut back on their guest list. It would be different if they were planning on splitting the cost with us —" the kitsune's mother narrowed her eyes and cocked her head — "no, no actually it wouldn't. Because that's not the day you want. But you need to start standing up to her now, Yuri, otherwise she's going to ride ramshod over your entire marriage. Set the bar now, that's what I had to do with your be-be."

Grace was inclined to agree with the older kitsune, and as the two women murmured back and forth, she reflected on how many brides-to-be she'd met over the years, squirming over having conversations with their future in-laws. She wanted to interject that the problem was not this girl's future mother-in-law, it was that she and her fiancé needed to be a united front, to have each other's backs, and to not give each other the burden of arguing with the other's mother. *Not your place*, she reminded herself. When she'd casually inquired into the wedding flowers, she was relieved when the girl said they had put much care into the choosing of their flowers. Pink peonies and stephanotis, with fragrant branches of apricot blossoms, an auspicious beginning for their marriage.

Her own little hand-tie of Lily of the Valley had begun to droop a few days after her observatory date with the tall mothman, and was now being pressed between the pages of a book, several heavy cans stacked atop it. *A return to happiness.* Grace couldn't deny that she had woken up feeling very happy indeed, even if her pubic bone was currently complaining.

"If you don't mind my saying so," she interjected, keeping her tone as even as she could, "I was a wedding planner for years before I started working here, and in my experience, one hundred and fifty guests is a perfect size reception. Once you start to get into two and three hundred people, you don't even get to see everyone. You'll spend the whole night just moving from table to table thanking people for coming, and before you know it, your own reception is over. If you're able to stick to your original plan . . ."

She let her voice trail off as she shrugged, the kitsune's mother harrumphing in triumph. When they left a short while later, the girl's head was held a bit higher, her mother still talking a mile a minute, the reception barn booked for the country-chic wedding she had planned.

As soon as they were out of sight, she'd slumped over the table, burying her own head in her arms, as the co-workers who'd been anxiously hovering around the reception area during the meeting descended on the coffee machine. A hot shower had been calling her name, as was her bed. *You should cut out early today. You put in enough long nights lately. One of the girls from the shop can sit at the table and play on their phone all afternoon.*

Within a matter of minutes, the circular concrete pad was overcrowded, the percolator nearly drained dry, Brogan and Zeke laughing loudly over a joke she'd not heard, and coming across the gravel walk, Caleia beelining towards her table. *You definitely should've called off today. Dumb bitch-itis strikes again.* Before Caleia could start her third degree, Cal came clip clopping in from the direction of the farm stand shop.

"Well, well," he smirked down. "Burning the midnight oil, aren't we?"

"Meeting go well, Cal?" piped up Quay, the slim tiefling who tended the sheep, sparing her from the centaur's loaded smile. "Last night?"

"Meetings went well. The agricultural department has some interesting ideas on what we can do to increase diversity in the orchards. We'll need to drop some new plans for the fields, it's probably too late for this year, but there are some smaller things we can do, he said. I want some of the parsley and dill transplanted over into the —"

He began to rattle off the increased duties the different divisions of labor would be handling, his voice becoming a blurring white noise, unimportant as she bent to retrieve the pen she'd dropped, feeling a sharp twinge of soreness.

"Caterpillars destroy crops, Cal," Brogan interjected roughly, his tone bringing her back to attention.

"Apparently if we plant rows of the things they prefer to feed on, they'll leave the actual crops alone. 'Butterfly bumps', he called them."

"So we're supposed to completely redo our crop schematics to *encourage* caterpillars? Most farms are spraying for pests, and we're going to roll out a welcome mat and offer them a twelve course feast?" Brogan and another field worker scoffed, sending a protective shiver rippling up her back at the *he* they were discussing.

"I can *sell* that, Cal. Do you have any idea what a draw butterfly gardens are?" She hadn't meant for her voice to be as hot as it was as heads swung at her sharp tone. "We can call the curriculum director for the schools, let her know that we'll have an on-site observation field for the kids. School field trips to observe the chrysalis stages, a walk-through garden in the spring, our own butterflies for weddings—no more having to special order them!"

"Little cups of nectar for people to feed the butterflies, a photo booth...I can put together a whole life-cycle segment for the schools," Caleia added, turning her venomous glare to the mumbling farmhands.

"There's an Arboretum upstate," Grace went on excitedly, struck by sudden inspiration. "They have a butterfly garden and a hummingbird garden. You can walk right through and see hundreds of little bumblebee-size hummingbirds zooming around, they don't even care about people. They're all feeding off the flowers. They do a program on insects, it's geared for kids, but my mom and I walked through it the last time I was home to visit. There are information stations on the sort of insects that feed off of different plants, and then you walk through the gardens, obviously, and they sell seedlings of the different plant varieties at the end of it. I'll run some figures this afternoon and get an idea of what their footsteps look like when the program is live."

"I can mock up some graphics," Caleia quickly added. We already have dill and parsley and whatever else you're talking about for sale in the shop, we can tailor the display around what we're already selling."

"Think about what that could do for the apiary," mused a tiefling from the farm stand. "We have a hard time moving the bigger containers, no one wants that sixteen-ounce monster, but if there was a program on how we are helping our native honeybees, I'll bet we would be able to get them sold. Especially if we do little gift baskets, I can have some of the girls put them together. The big bottle of honey, one or two of the plants ya'll are talking about, a few packets of flower seeds . . ." Grace and Caleia whirled in triumph, so in sync it could have been a choreographed move.

"All right!" the big centaur laughed. "You don't need to keep on selling the idea, I was already on board with it last night. Knew I could count on you ladies to turn it into an opportunity. You know," he went on, cantering over to the table, "if you'd have told me it was your boyfriend coming by, I might not have given him such a hard time."

She felt the weight of Caleia's eyes boring into the side of her head, but to her credit, her friend remained silent as Callum chuckled. The heat that flamed up her face was a curious mix of embarrassment — Callum was her boss, after all; she had no idea what he might have seen or overheard the night before, if he'd been outside his cottage when she'd left the farm, and she certainly didn't want to be the subject of idle gossip, already being the odd-human-out—and a tingling warmth, the thought of calling Merrick her *boyfriend* twisting her insides into a pleasant knot. *What's wrong with you? You can't go falling for him, not when you know he's leaving.*

"I'm pretty sure she'd have given him an even harder time, Cal. Which reminds me — we're trying to cultivate a welcoming, community-driven image. You yelling at visitors isn't helping to develop that."

Pushing to her feet, she swallowed down a groan, feeling dampness at her thighs, wondering if she'd ever stop *leaking,* before turning to the small office trailer, Caleia hot at her heels.

"Spill it," the petite dryad demanded, the instant the door clicked shut. All she wanted was a few moments to herself, to wipe herself clean for the hundredth time that morning and maybe curl up under her desk where she'd be undisturbed, but Caleia gracefully seated herself in the opposite chair, making herself comfortable.

"The guy you went out with is the one who came to the farm?! I want to hear *everything*, and don't you dare leave out a single detail!"

"You're really not going to let this go, right?"

"Oh, absolutely not. There is literally nothing I will hold onto longer, and your lifespan is very, very short compared to mine, just remember that."

Caleia's words made her sit up, frowning. "I never think of things like that, until you go and bring it up. How long do different species live for, anyway? Is that something to teach you in nymph school?"

The dryad laughed, a shimmering sound, as she shook out her long, shiny hair. "Actually, I think most of you have pretty commensurate lifespans. Minotaurs, orcs, goblins, humans. Trolls live a bit longer, satyrs also. Nymphs don't live as long as elves, not anymore, but still — it's a lot longer than the rest of you."

"What about mothmen?" she demanded, earning Caleia's gimlet-eyed smile.

"They're probably in that human-adjacent category. Now . . . Spill. It."

Grace almost felt guilty for wasting time on the clock as she recounted both her first and second date with Merrick, knowing her friend well enough to know that she would not, in fact, ever let it go. She wasn't sure of her descriptions of him were completely accurate — after all, she didn't want him to sound completely socially inept, only mentioning that he was a bit anxious and awkward, with an adorable stammer and wildly expressive antennae.

"It's so cute," she giggled, "I can tell when he's feeling nervous because his antennae drop down around his ears, and when he's excited they bobble around." She closed her eyes briefly, imagining his feathery antennae dancing around as he talked about his bats and hummingbirds, the way they'd stood on end as she'd sucked the tip of his writhing tentacle -like cock. He was adorable, and that was all Caleia needed to know.

"So let me get this straight. He's asleep right now, right?"

"I'm assuming so? He said that he starts his days in the late afternoon?"

"So you worked a full day yesterday and never even went home. He went over to his house in the evening after his meeting with Cal, he proceeds to fuck you senseless for the next sixteen hours or whatever –"

"It wasn't that long! Do you even know how to count?"

"He fucks you senseless," Caleia plowed on, undeterred, "presumably he gets his rocks off, and now he's snuggled up in bed while you're here, back at work, walking around bowlegged, dripping mothman jizz. Is that the jist of it?"

Grace sat back, defeated. "Yeah. Yeah, that pretty much sums it up. I think I'm going to go home early."

Caleia snorted. "You're an idiot for coming in at all. Was it at least worth not getting any sleep? Tell me he was at least good."

She dropped her head on the desk with a thud, wincing at the headache that had begun brewing behind her eye sometime during the wedding consultation. "He was *so* good. It was criminal. When I tell you I have never had a man go down on me like that. It was like he was on death row and I was his last meal. He does this suction thing with his tongue and —" she trailed off, her clit quivering at the memory of what he'd done to it. "And his cock is like . . . I don't know, nothing I've ever seen before. It hit *all* the right places. And he had never been with a human before! He could have been a virgin for all I know! I could have taken this sweet mothman's virginity last night, Caleia. Do you know what kind of responsibility that is? Every bone in my body feels bruised, I'm exhausted, and my head is pounding, but if he were to call me right now and ask if he could come over to eat me out again the way he did last night, I'd be sitting in my front yard with my legs open waiting for him."

They had both collapsed into giggles when the trailer door swung open, the tiefling from the farm stand popping her head in to borrow a file folder.

"Okay, so he eats pussy like a champ, he's very sweet and smart, you're obviously attracted to him. Why do I feel like there's a 'but' coming on? This is exactly the kind of guy you need! He's nothing like your ex, you just said so. So what's the problem?"

"He's probably not going to be around for long," she sighed. "He's here on a research fellowship through the University, and once the program ends or the funding is cut, he'll be on his way. He's moved around a lot from the sound of it."

"Well shit. What's the plan then? You gonna cut him loose?"

Grace closed her eyes again, trying to imagine breaking things off with the sweet, stammering mothman. She'd never survived the conversation, the sound of those little clicks and disappointed chirps would do her in.

"No. He's so sweet, and I really do like him. Anyway, we've only been out twice. He might be a total asshole, you know? I just haven't found out yet."

"You're planning on finding out then?"

She hesitated for a long moment. It would be easy to walk away, easy and probably smart . . . But the thought of doing so twisted her lungs, the notion that she'd not hear those little chirps again leaving her feeling hollow.

"I'm planning on showing him around town and enjoying his company for as long as he's here. I know not to risk my heart, but he's so far he's been sweet and funny, and I would be a fool to say no to having his face between my legs for as long as he's willing to put it there."

She left work a short while later, pleading a headache in the bright sunlight. Cal had waved her off, telling her to start the weekend early, and he'd see her on Monday. She'd spent a mortifying thirty minutes in her bathroom, squatting over the tub and bearing down with all her might, attempting to expel as much of his dripping seed as she could. She would never have let him finish inside her, she grumbled to herself as she dripped on the porcelain, had she known he was going to leave her sloshing with a gallon of moth cum, but it was too late for self recrimination.

Live and learn. She was on birth control and a niggling little voice in her head told her he was fairly inexperienced. *So you're a little sloshy today. Aren't you happy knowing you were able to make him come that hard? You'll live.*

When at last she climbed into her own bed, Grace considered everything that had transpired over the last 24 hours. Reaching for her phone, she scrolled until she reached his name. Merrick. She liked the sight of it there, and wondered if he kept the same number, regardless of where he lived at any given time.

"Your Cambric Creek sightseeing adventure starts this weekend. I was thinking first on the list would be the waterfall and Main Street. Are you free Saturday night?" She set the phone face down on her bedside table, knowing it would be hours before he responded. Snuggling into her pillow, she tugged the summer weight blanket up over her shoulders. She was going to learn something new about mothmen, she was going to show him around, they were going to have a ton of great sex, and they were going to have a good time.

It doesn't matter how long he's going to be around. You can still have fun. Just don't go falling in love and you'll be fine. Closing her eyes, she ran the tips of her fingers over her forearm, trying not to notice the way she'd woken up that morning covered in a fine layer of his wing dust, soft and silky, dust she'd endeavored not to brush off all morning. A perfect cocoon of him, wrapped around her as she drifted to sleep.

Eight

"So the werewolves and shifters get along here?"

It was the second time he'd asked the question, still dubious of her affirmation. They were standing on the overlook, looking down at the crashing water, the town's titular creek meandering through residential yards and parks until it tumbled over the rock face in the middle of downtown in a lovely, dramatic display. They were eating ice cream from an old-fashioned little ice cream parlor that was on the square. She'd sheepishly admitted to never having visited the shop before as they crossed the threshold, arm-in-arm.

"But I've been to their scoop truck a bunch of times, at the Maker's Mart. It's every Saturday morning, right over there in the municipal lot. You're going to have to come visit me at my table, I sign up CSA subscriptions, and one of the girls from the farmstand sells foodstuff."

"This is all so . . . idyllic. It's almost creepy. I keep waiting for the other shoe to drop. There has to be some weird cult or something, right? Everything is very crunchy and collaborative, but then someone gets sacrificed in the town square every third full moon to keep everyone happy, is that it?"

She dissolved into giggles, batting at his arm playfully.

"No! Yes, the werewolves and shifters get along here. No, there are no cult sacrifices! I can't help it if you only ever lived in the city and aren't used to small town living."

"It's not that I only lived in cities, far from it," he shrugged, devouring the rest of his cone. "I'm just not used to people being *nice*. It's weird."

Grace glanced over at him, expecting to see him grinning in jest, frowning when he seemed completely serious.

She had met him at the school, where he gave her a short tour of the facility he worked in. She'd hardly been able to pay attention to the lab they walked through or the tanks of convalescing animals they passed in an outdoor section. All she could focus on was the sight of him in his lab coat. It was a typical lab coat, nothing unusual or exceptional about it, and that was what was so disturbing. It was the same lab coat a human might've worn, worn backwards over his arms, leaving his wings free. His name was stitched over the area that should have been the back of the right shoulder, hitting him on the upper left side of his chest. He had modified the front, cutting down the center so that he wasn't choked by the collar, and she was discomfited at the sight of him wearing it.

"They give you that when you started here?" she'd asked casually, as they'd walked back to his office, gesturing to the lab coat.

"Hmm? Oh, no, this is mine. From two facilities ago, I think? I'll probably need a new one soon, they fray pretty quickly, unfortunately. I should probably have one fixed up after I cut down the front, to keep the unfinished hem from unraveling."

He seemed to think nothing of having a coat that was not designed for his body type, for his species, one that barely fit him and had to be cut open just to accommodate his thick mantle of fluff. She didn't like the uncomfortable creep of *knowing* when she imagined how he must've been treated at his previous places of employment.

The handful of times she and the girls went to dinner in Bridgeton, Grace would leave the restaurant wondering if she'd not been present, if they would've been served at all. The city teemed with goblins and trolls, satyrs and orcs filling in the gaps, but they seemed oddly invisible in predominantly human settings, and she wondered if that's how he had always existed in his labs.

"I think a new lab coat is an excellent idea," she said decisively, but he'd seemed oblivious, and they'd left the campus shortly after.

"I already told you, werewolves and shifters founded the town together. There was a group of founding families, and they ran everything for decades. Only two of them are left, for the most part, and of the two, only one is still in any sort of position of power. One of them is probably going to be the new mayor soon."

"And they don't mind that orcs and goblins moved into the town they started? Are you *sure*? Did someone ask them?"

Grace pressed her lips together, giving him a *look*, and he chuckled again, rich and low in response. He seemed determined to poke holes in her assertion that Cambric Creek was welcoming to all species, unlike the mostly human towns and cities and villages where he'd previously been employed.

"I'm just asking!"

"*No*," she huffed, trying not to smile as he continued to laugh. "I've already told you a hundred times. No, they don't care."

When they'd stepped through the doors of the ice cream parlor, her eyes had gone up to the board, looking over the dozens and dozens of flavors listed. She had no idea what a mothman might enjoy, unsure if she ought to make suggestions or not.

"Oh . . . oh look, they have aphid mint! That sounds interesting. I wonder what's in that."

Merrick cocked an eyebrow, looking at her askance.

"I'm assuming it has aphids. And mint. Probably for the amphibians. Is-is that what you're going to order?" She'd squeaked her protest, and he'd barely been able to hide his twitching smile. "Who knows? Might be good. You should try it if it caught your eye, Grace."

They were next in line at that point, the cheerful goblin behind the counter asking if they had made up their minds on their flavors.

"I'm going to have the non dairy caramel crunch, single scoop, waffle cone. My beautiful companion here is contemplating the aphid mint, but I have a feeling she's going to go with something else."

She had been as red as a tomato when they'd walked out of the shop, her cherry chocolate chip cone already beginning to drip.

"Aphid mint," he'd shaken his head, snorting in laughter as she swatted at his arm.

"How was I supposed to know!" she'd whined. "I'm your first human, but you're my first mothman! I don't know what you eat! I just wanted you to order something you'd be comfortable with!"

". . . Aphid mint!"

If nothing else, her faux pas had broken the ice of the afternoon, and her fingers had been knitted securely with his since then. They'd walked the length of the towpath, following the meandering Creek to the waterfall's overlook, where they now stood.

"Fruit, grains, nuts, legumes. What I eat, I mean. You can get a lot of protein from non-meat sources, you know. I definitely don't need aphids."

"What about veggies?!"

His head turned slowly to face her, his red eyes narrowing. Her eyebrows shot up, unsure of what she had said that was controversial enough to earn such a reaction.

"Vegetables are a myth, Grace. There's no classification for vegetables in botany, because it doesn't exist. What we call vegetables are just edible parts of plants that have their own botanical taxonomy."

She understood the concept of what he was saying, for it had been discussed on the farm numerous times. Several of the employees of the farmstand often went rounds with Brogan and several of the others over what they classified as fruits and what were labeled as vegetables in the shop, but she had never heard any of them argue that vegetables were a *myth*.

"A myth. Like Bigfoot?" He scowled and she almost choked on her laughter, burying her face against his side as her shoulders shook. "You should see your face!" she howled. "You're so serious!"

"You're overlooking my favorite food," he growled, tugging her close. "I have a new favorite meal. I'd like to incorporate it into a weekly part of my diet, if I'm able." His tongue had dropped from his mouth, its coil unspooling until it was able to slip between her breasts, and she felt a flutter of excitement between her thighs.

"Well, that's important," she breathed, feeling the tip of the coil push beneath the lace of her bra, curl around her nipple and tug. "You should enjoy what you eat."

They'd wound up back at her house, where he laid her out on her bed before covering her with his wide wings, his mouth closing over her cunt, showing his *appreciation* for his new favorite food. He'd not allowed her to tease his cock out that day, insisting that he couldn't stay, but she'd orgasmed twice against his hungry mouth, stimulating her until she was no longer capable of words, leaving her a boneless puddle when she came against his tongue. Her clit was still pulsing when he kissed her, leaving her there in a heap on her bed, to go back to work.

When she was capable of movement again, Grace reached out for her cell phone. She opened her notes app, beginning a new file. *Things I have learned about mothmen. Obsessed with eating pussy. Very serious opinions about vegetables. Vibrating cocks. No aphids.* She let the phone drop to the mattress as her eyes closed, deciding a little nap would not be amiss.

It would be hard working around their respective schedules, she realized. Unless she could learn to be happy with late afternoon dates, or else pre-dawn dalliances. She didn't expect that he would be able to pull away whenever she wanted him to during the work week, and she knew she didn't have that sort of flexibility at the farm, but . . . they could make it work. *It's only temporary,* she reminded herself. *He's not going to be around forever, so you may as well enjoy the time you have together.* She drifted to sleep, thinking of aphids, wondering how they felt about being a protein supplement in someone else's dessert, and if anyone had ever considered their opinion on the matter.

"Grace, you have a visitor," Caleia called out in a singsong voice.

She flushed, not expecting to see him, certainly not expecting to see him that early in the day. In the bright afternoon sunlight, his velutinous skin looked brown; a warm nutty color, and the change intrigued her.

"You look completely different like this!" she'd exclaimed, not rising from her table. His feathery antennae was flattened around his pointed ears, his guarded eyes flickering nervously to the dryad who hovered pointedly at the edge of the table. "Merrick, this is Caleia. She's the farm's record keeper. She was a big help getting Cal to agree to your program. Caleia," she threw her friend a venomous look of warning, "this is Merrick. He's a scientist from the University."

To her credit, Caleia managed to act as if she'd not heard of the tall moth before, certainly didn't know anything about his bedroom habits, and had absolutely *not* received a painstakingly detailed description of the way he'd ejaculated on her breasts a few days earlier.

He didn't work in his lab on weekends, and she had arranged to not be stuck at her table past the end of her normal workday, freeing their evenings Friday through Sunday. It was hard to believe more than a month had passed since that first night at the observatory, but time always flew in the summertime.

They had visited Applethorpe Manor, the expansive gardens of which he'd already seen in his initial work visit to the grounds. The ghillie dhu who was employed as the chief horticulturist at the manor house had been resistant to Merrick's suggestions for how the manor might improve its pollinator friendliness, a fact he didn't share with her until they were already midway through their tour of the house. They'd run into the ghillie dhu a short while later as they walked through the topiary garden. The tall, green-skinned man had scowled in recognition, and it had been all she could do to keep her laughter in check until they were well out of earshot.

"You really *are* a lab coat know-it-all!" She giggled, hunching over. "Look at that! Did you see that *look*?! That dude hates you!"

Her fact of the day had been an interesting revelation about the typical mating rituals of mothpeople.

"We don't really have sex more than once or twice a month, not normally," he'd explained sheepishly, when he'd again declined letting her arouse him until his cock slid free. "It takes . . . you know, a *while*."

She did, in fact, know what he meant. She'd begun to fear that her cervix was being physically displaced every time they had intercourse, and the length of time it took for him to ejaculate, which meant the length of time he spent fucking her, was far longer than her body could keep up with.

"I don't want you to be unsatisfied because you're worried about hurting me," she'd fretted that evening, leading to his hesitant explanation.

"Even married couples won't have intercourse more than a few times a month, and it's practically a twenty-four hour event. I don't have time for that. Don't worry, I'm more than satisfied."

She'd been surprised, but somewhat relieved. Merrick's endless, insatiable tongue kept her well-satisfied in the weeks leading up to the days when he was in the mood for intercourse, and she didn't have to face a future of being bow-legged and sore indefinitely, even if that future was only for the interim.

For his part, he seemed happy with their arrangement. He loved going down on her, that hadn't changed; was completely addicted to the taste of her slick, still comparing her to the sweetness of the blackberries they'd shared that very first night. She quickly learned that his favorite two foods could easily be classified into those two columns — sweet, ripe berries, and her slippery slick cunt, which he claimed was just as sweet. On the occasions that he *did* want to fuck, she had learned his appetite was equally ravenous. He could rut her for hours, moaning in pleasure the whole time — changing positions, holding her suspended over his arms they hovered several feet off the ground, his hips thrusting upwards like a train piston.

The day they'd visited the manor house had been one such occasion. He was still just as anxious and awkward when they were out in public, especially if there were large groups of people, the fact that so many species actively lived and worked and loved together was still a foreign concept for him, but behind closed doors, his bashfulness was quickly forgotten.

They'd barely been back in his tree loft for a few minutes when he'd placed her hand directly on his slit. She had learned over the course of the last month that Merrick could be reduced to a pile of jelly when she fingered the slit in his skin, exactly the same way he fingered her cunt. His breathing would grow labored when she pressed her fingers into the opening, hips bucking up into her when she added more than one, and she decided that he deserved a nice, slow buildup that evening.

He was hot, and she could feel the slight bulge of his cock beneath, anxious to come out. She'd taken her time teasing him — fingering his slit slowly, swirling her fingers in his viscous lubrication, rubbing the interior wall and reveling in its slippery smooth texture and the way he quivered from within. When she'd added a second finger, he'd wheezed. She was able to grip the very tip of his cock from where it still lay nestled within his body, tickling at it and trapping it between her fingertips until it had surged forward.

He liked her hands on him, he liked her mouth on him, he liked the squeeze of being inside her. She got him to admit that he was attracted to humans, even if he'd always been invisible in their midst at his job, and Grace suspected he was acting out long-held fantasies with her.

He liked to hold the round swells of her hips, like kissing each of her toes and the arch of her foot, so unlike his own insectoid hindquarters. But what he liked the most, she'd learned as the weeks passed, aside from burying his face between her thighs, was the softness of her breasts. He would hold their weight in his palms, thumbs circling over her nipples, squeezing and pinching until they puckered and hardened under his ministrations. She had wondered privately if there had been a human coworker at one point with breasts at least as large as hers, if not bigger, someone he'd fantasized over, invisible and unnoticed in his backwards lab coat. She wondered if he had masturbated over his human kink before, if it was the fact that she was human that had made him stop outside her window in the first place.

He'd enjoyed her teasing, and once his cock had fully distended, Grace had another idea. She would never say no when he wanted to have intercourse, not for as often as he pleasured her in those days and weeks in between, but she had a busy few days ahead of her, and didn't fancy the idea of being bow legged and sore for most of them.

Grace considered, as she settled on a cushion at his feet, once she'd tugged him to sit in his specially-designed chair, that she had been an anxious mess three scant years ago, yet here she was, a brazen seductress on her knees. Merrick's garnet eyes were scrunched shut as she stroked the curving length of his cock, and he never saw her pick up the wand.

The magic wand had never been a favorite toy. She'd bought it because of the cult hype surrounding it, but it was too heavy, too powerful, and numbed her more than it got her off. It had been in a bag of toys she'd brought with her to his tree loft, giving him something to use on her on the nights where intercourse was not on the menu.

It would, however, be perfect to use on him. The large, conical head whirred to life, and she raised it to that big bottom swell, the reason she was usually so sore the morning after what she had begun to mentally refer to as Fuck Nights, where he was so sensitive. Merrick yelped, his hips lifting as though he'd been electrocuted, but she followed his movements, keeping the buzzing vibrator against his curving length.

For the next fifteen minutes, she learned where to hold the wand. Moving down his cock-tip proved to be too much, and the high-pitched noise he made, so different from his normal deep purr, might have been comical if she weren't on a mission. Following the S-shaped line of him made him groan, and pressed to his flared base made him pant. The bottom swell still elicited the longest moans, but pressing the vibrator's head to his slit made him arch off the chair, and she wondered how deeply it was stimulating him.

When she clicked the vibrator off, a strangled *kreeee* ripped from his throat, and she almost fell over laughing. She ignored the peevish look he gave her when she climbed into the chair, straddling his hips. His eyes fluttered shut when she guided the dripping tip of him into her, slowly sinking down on his length until she reached that heavy bottom swell.

"I don't think I can get over this on my own," she panted, feeling the familiar burn.

His face scrunched, sucking in a deep breath as she wobbled in place astride him.

"I-I don't want to hurt you, I don't want you to be uncomfortable. This is fine, this is enough."

Grace scowled at the return of his stammer, tapping him on the nose. "If I wanted your bad opinions, I would have asked for them. Just thrust up a little, help me get over this." He obliged her tentatively, and on the third upward thrust of his hips, she was able to sink over the swell, the air in her lungs leaving her in a gasp. "Tell me about the guy from the garden, the one at the Manor house. What did you argue about?"

Expecting him to keep his composure enough to have a conversation while she cock warmed him was simply asking too much, as he quickly displayed. She continued to ask questions, prodding him to remain engaged in the conversation as she rocked her hips against him slowly, barely moving, tightening her inner muscles to squeeze him.

"That guy was a real asshole," he gritted out through clenched teeth. "I told him I'd seen a friendlier set-up at the elementary school, I guess he didn't appreciate that."

She'd been wheezing in laughter against his chest, certain that there had probably been two assholes involved in that particular conversation, when he'd pushed himself out of the chair, obliging her to wrap her legs around his waist with a squeak. He was as ravenous as ever, but the vibrator had done a good job at speeding things along. By the time he'd been ready to erupt, she was pleased to note she didn't feel as though her organs had been displaced in his frenzy.

"Do you want to come on my tits?"

She was certain he had a human kink, a breast kink in particular when he moaned his agreement. She resumed her place on her knees before him, squeezing her breasts together as he came like a geyser, a spray of his pearly release coating her skin in seconds. It was thinner than what she was used to, especially compared to the thick, creamy consistency of a minotaur's, and there was *so* much of it, but when it was finally over, and she knelt in a puddle, it was clear he'd enjoyed himself. *Let him take that memory with him wherever he goes next,* she thought, as he fretted over cleaning her up.

Seeing him now, under the bright afternoon sun was incongruous, but certainly welcome.

"I-I wasn't sure if you would be available to take lunch, if you're not, I totally – I-I should've called you first, I'm sorry, maybe later tonight we can, before I have to go in, maybe—"

"I would love to take lunch, actually. This is what time I usually go anyway."

A burst of small voices interrupted her next words, the Woodland Scouts who had visited the farm that day returning from the outer fields in a noisy cluster of uniformed little bodies.

"What do we say to Ms. Grace for getting us all set up today, gang?"

At the sound of the man's voice, she snapped to attention, pasting on her brightest, sunniest smile. Caleia had made herself invisible, retreating to the office trailer in a blur of movement, leaving Grace singularly responsible for saying goodbye to the town's next mayor, relieved that she'd taken Tris's advice, placing *Hemming for Mayor* sign at the entrance to the long drive, and if Cal had disliked it, he had the good sense not to say anything.

She'd previously met the handsome werewolf's genial brother, the fireman, on several different occasions, and had once stood in line at the Black Sheep behind another brother, his hands clasped with a petite, dark-haired young woman, getting their last caffeine fix before an apparent hiking trip, as Grace listened in intently to them reviewing their supply list.

She wasn't sure what she had been expecting when he had called to make the appointment for the Woodlands Scouts, but Jackson Hemming was younger looking than she'd antic-ipated, far younger than a mayor ought to look, she thought, with an odd intensity that made her squirm. He'd been a professor at the school, but had left his job at the end of the spring term, in preparation for the new job everyone in town expected him to have by the following year. He was just as handsome as his fireman brother, his eyes sparkling and his smile white and even, but there was something in his eyes, something slightly frenetic and all-seeing, and as the group of children thanked her in unison, Grace watched his overly-intense gaze slide to Merrick, traveling up the reedy moth's unclothed body slowly, the body she loved, his dark eyebrows drawing together in a brief expression of disapproval. His gaze had snapped back to hers a heartbeat later, and it happened so fast she may have been persuaded to think she'd imagined it, but she knew better.

"We were so thrilled to have you all! Any time you want to come back, just say the word!"

She'd sagged into her seat once they were gone, Caleia's head popping out of the trailer door. "Is it safe?"

Grace scowled at the cowardly dryad, shaking her head in disgust.

"For that, you get to come over here and pop a squat. We're going to lunch, and it's probably going to be a late one." She turned to Merrick, giving him a tremulous smile, noting that his antennae had lowered a bit. "C'mon. We're going to get lunch and then we are going to introduce you to the fabulous new world of *pants*."

Chapter Nine

Nine

"This is a nice place."

Grace lifted her head, eyebrow raised at his words. She'd grown used to sleeping cuddled against his chest on his chair, as she did then. She wasn't sure how long she had been dozing, nor what had prompted his statement in the first place, but she grinned at his contemplative tone.

A full two months had passed since their very first date, perhaps a bit longer, she realized when she considered how much of the summer had already passed. She'd taken him to all of her favorite restaurants, to hear live music in the gazebo on weekend evenings, another trip to the observatory and actual stargazing in his loft, to the Maker's Mart on Saturday mornings, and to a free concert put on by the community choir. He'd marveled at the adaptive architecture of the different neighborhoods, expressing his appreciation for how seriously so many of the area businesses he visited for his program were taking the initiative he'd laid out. It had been the nicest summer she could remember experiencing since childhood, and the thought that it would soon be drawing to a close was a dark shadow on her heart.

That night, the entry in her note app was once again about food. Specifically, the mothman appetite. Her mothman, at least. They'd had meal plans for that evening — a late dinner for her and brunch for him, but then he'd been needed to fill in over in the classrooms and she'd wound up working late. By the time they were both free, it was nearly the middle of the night, and he'd still not eaten. She could tell he was sulking, deciding to remind him of the benefits of living in the multispecies town.

"C'mon, let's go get you some food. The Food Gryphon is open all night, let's get you some fruit. We can make big salads."

"I'm too hungry," he grumbled. "Besides, it's the middle of the night. You should be asleep."

Grace rolled her eyes, replacing her short nightgown with a t-shirt dress.

"First of all, it's the weekend, and I'm not one of your hummingbirds. I'll sleep when I want, bossy. And seriously, you're too hungry to *go and get* food?"

Less than ten minutes later, they were touching down in the parking lot of the grocery store. She would never enjoy flying, Grace had determined. She clung to him the entire time they were in the air, her face buried again his fluff, hoping he couldn't hear her occasional screams.   "C'mon," she cajoled, stroking his velvety arm. The parking lot was nearly full, despite the late hour, and she watched as a family of humanoid bats cross through the automatic doors. "We'll get all your favorites."

"I think I'm too weak to go in. They'll probably have to carry me out on a stretcher."

She bit her lip, holding back a smile in the face of his petulance. Merrick was calm and aggravatingly rational most of the time, but she'd discovered he had a particular talent for poutiness. His feathery antennae twitched as he scowled down at her smile.

"I'm just trying to avoid you having to spend the night in the emergency room when my stomach tries to digest my lungs. You're welcome."

The Food Gryphon was open twenty-four hours a day, catering to the vast array of residents who called Cambric Creek home. As Merrick pulled a cart from the corral, after begrudgingly following her in, she eavesdropped on a vampire couple, arguing over a bottle of wine.

"Why do we need to spend this much? No one is even going to drink it!"

"Do you want Doctor Resanovic to think we're cheapskates? Use your head, Byron."

Before her, the produce aisle stretched, long and green and plentiful, and she sighed in relief.

"Did you know that the starvation process starts in as little as seventy-two hours? Pretty soon my brain will have depleted its glucose stores and my liver will need to start converting amino acids just to keep me alive."

The vampires raised their heads to stare in unison as Merrick gave an enormous sigh, and she glared.

"Well it's a good thing you haven't actually gone seventy-two hours without eating. Look, they have everything! Let's get our salad stuff and go, I'll bet the lines are terrible for as crowded as the parking lot was."

"I'm in danger of an electrolyte imbalance, you know. I can feel the autophagy already ravaging my muscles."

Now the vampires were whispering, and she wondered what kind of doctor their Doctor Resanovic was. *They're probably going to call him, let him know there's a moth dying of starvation in the grocery store.*

"They have a whole endcap of frozen pizzas right over there, Grace. You should just get yourself one with extra pepperoni and leave me in the parking lot. Putrefaction will set in within a few days, there won't even be anything left of me to clean up."

The vampires clutched each other's hands, their argument over the wine forgotten.

"Gosh, that's too bad. Fuck Night is on this week's calendar, and now you're planning on dying here in front of the onions." A series of outraged clicks accompanied his huff as she turned away, not bothering to hide her smile.

Kale, spinach, mesclun. Blueberries, blackberries, strawberries . . . Merrick was finally quiet as she piled the cart, trailing a few steps behind her, and she hoped he was mollified by the abundance of fruit. The vampires were now bickering over the necessity of papaya on the fruit tray for their dinner party, and she wondered how much they were going to spend on food that wouldn't be eaten.

A flickering motion from the corner of her eye made her turn sharply, but there was nothing other than a heap of over-priced cherries next to the grapes. She had moved as far as the mountain of limes at the end of the aisle when it happened again.

She turned to face her companion, but he was still pushing the cart, hands firmly wrapped around the handlebar. *Something is off* . . . she stared, realizing after a moment what was different.

Merrick was chewing.

As she turned back to the produce, she kept him in her peripheral vision, watching in amused horror as his long, coiled tongue unfurled, wrapping around a plump, green grape. His hands never moved and he remained upright, the picture of innocence. The grape vanished and he chirped happily, antennae bobbing.

"Merrick! Are you stealing fruit?!"

"I'm checking it for aphids! You know, you're too used to the fruit on the farm, you have no idea what could be infecting this imported stuff. Did you know an entire town died from a single spider in a banana?" A cherry was his next victim, then another, and he chirped once more, his mantle puffing up as he hummed.

"That's an urban legend!" she snapped, glancing around. One of the store employees had appeared, pushing a cart of apples in front of her, and the vampires were straining to overhear her conversation behind. *Trapped. Definitely time to go.* "You are incorrigible! Let's get out of here, those vampires are watching you. I didn't realize I was sleeping with a criminal!"

Now she pressed against his chest, listening to the happy near purr he emitted, his stomach full and her head heavy, at last ready for sleep. It was the happiest summer she could ever remember having, and she wasn't ready for it to be over. Autumn had been all she was looking forward to, and now its whisper hung in the air like a portent, the sun sinking in the horizon earlier and earlier each night, signaling the end of the season drawing near.

Her meeting with the head of the community boards planning committee had gone as smoothly as if she had scripted it — a beautifully sunny day without a cloud in the sky, the heat abating slightly, at least for that morning, all of the farm's employees on their very best behavior. The werecat had been impressed with her background in venue management and wedding planning, was mollified at the size of the southernmost lot and the additional area they would allocate for parking, surveying the fields where vendors would sell their wares and carnival rides would be erected for the long weekend festival.

When it had all been over, they had gone out to celebrate, back to Gildersnood, and she'd felt a little ripple of déjà vu. Going home that night to her empty house had felt all-too-familiar, and when she pulled her dress over her head, climbing to the center of her back, she thumbed open her phone, letting her audience know that the curtain was about to go up.

He was far from perfect, she had learned. Awkward and anxious, but also arrogant and assuming. He was passionate about his work, passionate about what he did, and his people skills were distant second, but she'd also learned that her first instincts had proven correct — he was very sweet, very considerate, and the soft sound of his chirps and clicks and filled in the gaps of her world that she'd scarcely been aware of until his presence in their place.

She'd nearly missed the soft *whump* in the tree outside her window, the branches thick and heavy with leaves. All too soon they would begin to turn; green to gold, to red and orange, dropping from the branches the same way he would eventually drop out of her life, as unexpectedly as he'd dropped into it.

As her hands moved down her body, gliding over the soft curves he enjoyed so much, she wondered what she would do when he was gone. She'd gone and fallen in love, against her better judgment, even though she knew it was foolish. She'd not protected her heart as well as she had intended, and it would hurt when he left, a scoop of her heart that he would permanently take with him. It would probably hurt worse than when she had run away, she realized, for all she had been running away from *was* hurt.

The love had died in her marriage years before she'd left, but this love was fresh, a recent brand on her heart. She shouldn't have let him in so deeply, shouldn't have spent so much time in his company and in his bed, but saying such a thing, even *thinking* such a thing felt wrong. She had met him and she had fallen in love, and she was glad for it, because it meant she was still able to do such a thing. She would miss him terribly when he was gone and her heart would unquestionably be broken, but Grace couldn't find it in her to wish that she'd done anything different.

Her fingers had found their way into her slick center that night of her triumphant meeting, and she performed for him the same way she'd done that night several months earlier. When his flickering tongue met her heated skin, it was no longer a foreign sensation. Familiar and pleasurable, touched with tenderness, she thought. When he began to suck her, her head dropped back, surrendering to the sensation. This was his favorite thing to do, she could deny him nothing. If he'd noticed the tears that ran down her face as she came against the suction of his tongue, he was considerate enough not to mention them.

"It's a very nice place, of course it is. That's why I love living here so much."

He had let himself into her house early the previous morning, shortly after the sky had begun to lighten with the dawn, and his agitated excitement had been so palpable, she'd woken up to see what he was pacing around over. The lab coat was designed for a winged species, slipped over the arms the way one would wear a normal garment, with Velcro sections that were left opened to accommodate wings, fastened once the wearer had pulled it on.

"Look what they did!" he'd exclaimed, his hands trembling with the adrenaline of such a gift. "Look what they got for me!"

He had never owned an item of adaptive clothing, she'd discovered the day she'd taken him shopping. All the clothes he'd owned had been created for humans, things he'd been forced to cut and modify, never actually fitting his long, angular body. If he'd been surprised by the other nocturnal and crepuscular employees at the school, the clothing stores that lined Main Street completely blew his mind. Shirts for people with multiple arms, saddle kilts for centaurs, pants designed for hooved and hocked residents. The pants they found him had been a touch a short, as he was uncommonly tall, but he'd marveled over the neat tucks that ended where his insectoid lower legs bent back. First pants, and now this lab coat. Grace could almost see his world getting larger, and she was glad she was there to witness it.

"Well, they must really like you. That's not surprising to hear, you're probably all a bunch of lab coat know-it-alls."

He'd stood in front of the mirror on the back of her closet door, examining himself in his new lab coat, wearing the pants they purchased for him, his nose scrunched.

"I don't know if I like this, Grace."

"Well, I do," she murmured, stretching up on her toes to kiss his sharp shoulder blade. "You look very handsome."

Her eyes fluttered open as she repeated that Cambric Creek was, in fact, a very nice place. The canopy was open, and above their heads a million and one stars winked in a cloudless sky. She was able to see flashes of lightning bugs beyond the netting around the balcony, the tree cover of the forest dense and black enough to blot out the light pollution from town. It was magical and soft, and although her heart would undoubtedly be broken when he left, there was nowhere else in the world she would choose to be.

CHAPTER TEN

Ten

HEA

Old habits, she was forced to admit, died terribly long, agonizingly protracted deaths.

She hadn't meant to assist the kitsune with her veil; had no intention of fixing several of the flower arrangements on the tables in the reception barn. She certainly hadn't meant to corral the bridesmaids or give last-minute instructions to the musicians. All she'd meant to do was ensure that Saddlethorne looked its best, that the reception barn was radiant, and that the caterers that had been hired in weren't having any logistical issues. Somehow she'd managed to do all of the above and then some.

The morning had started with a brief rain shower, just a light sprinkle, an auspicious beginning, she'd assured the bride once she'd arrived on site. The fields hadn't gotten muddy, and there was no permeating smell of wet animal in the air. Just a quick shower to ensure a happy marriage, and Grace had found herself wishing that she had been half as lucky. Caleia had been acting as her assistant since she'd arrived that morning, following behind her with checklists, and scurrying to fetch extra table cloths or farmhands to help move some of the heavier pieces of furniture without scratching the freshly waxed floors. The tables were set, the cake had been delivered, and the catering truck had arrived right on time.

The barn was strung with white twinkle lights, and Mason jars of favors graced each place setting. Long, rough-hewn benches lined the tables, with pale pink floral arrangements of roses and peonies perfuming the air. She was in the personal opinion that all of these farm themed weddings looked exactly the same, right down to the burlap ribbons on the Mason jars, but the bride was ecstatic with the way it all turned out, and Grace didn't mind giving herself a pat on the back for pulling it all off.

Cal had been in an exceptionally good mood since her meeting with the community board, and that day was no exception. His tartan was spotless, his smile genuine, and the ferocious gleam he normally displayed was muted for the event. The division of labor for an event like this often required more hands than the meager staff she had for events possessed, but Brogan and Zeke had pitched in, sending some of their own farmhands and assistants to aid in whatever Grace needed done. In all her years of wedding planning, she had never had an event go as smoothly as the kitsune's nuptials had started out, and she knew better than to assume things would stay that way.

"Did I tell you about that guy that was here the other day?" Caleia remarked casually, as they waited on the circular drive, anticipating the kitsune's arrival. "The guy with the birds?"

"The guy from the other day with the birds. Try being a little more vague, babe. I have no idea what you're talking about."

The nymph huffed. "He was from some university in South America, said he's an ornithologist. Birds, right? He was telling me all about a program he's starting for the fall semester at the University where he works, and it sounded really similar to the thing your boyfriend is doing here. I was telling him about Merrick. Anyway, I just thought it was a funny coincidence. This guy being all nervous about hummingbird conservation, and your cutie moth boy is always in a tizzy over bats or bees, or whatever it is he studies."

She'd turned to face Caleia sharply. It was easy to write off Merrick's program as being strictly about honey bees or butterflies, but she knew how devoted he was to the zooming little hummingbirds in his loft, could only imagine the care in which he'd nursed the little clutch of bats he'd told her about. It wasn't simply one or two animal species he was preoccupied with all the time, it was *all* of them, she'd learned. He fretted over ant colonies and grew agitated over the fate of an opossum he'd seen several times in her yard. That he'd been forced to narrow down his focus professionally had, she had no doubt, been the cause of an existential meltdown at the start of his academic career, but he'd probably not had a choice. He was just as interested in hummingbirds as this South American stranger was, but she held her tongue as Caleia continued.

"Anyway, this guy was really excited because his program just got funded, so he's trying to staff it right now. I wonder how many other weird jobs there are out there like that. You think there's someone whose entire job it is to just follow around like, bullfrogs and study their sleep cycle? It's crazy to think about!"

Black throated mangoes, they're native to South America. One of my colleagues there sent these to me. The world she knew and the life she had rebuilt for herself within it rocked beneath her feet. It was far too much of a coincidence, and she had never believed in coincidences. The summer semester was winding down, and Merrick had mumbled something about wondering if they would be funded to continue into the fall. Her heart had quavered at his words, and she'd not had the courage to push the issue then. Now this man was here, this man who studied the same thing he did, who had just been funded for a similar program. *Here for a good time, not a long time.*

Her face heated and her throat stuck, a telltale sign of tears, but she pushed them down. She had too much to focus on that day, and after all, she'd always known he would leave. Caleia had already moved on to a new topic of conversation, and Grace refocused on the day ahead of her. The bride would be arriving soon, the final check delivered, Cal's favorite part of the day, and she needed to make sure things went off without a hitch.

The day they had gone clothes shopping, the day he had received a sharp look over from Jackson Hemming, she'd nearly given up the game.

"Remind me again why this is all of a sudden a life or death situation? I had some supplies to drop off at the winery up the road, I just wanted to take you to lunch."

She'd turned, beaming. Much as he'd given the hard sell to Cal, Merrick had somehow managed to convince grouchy old Enoch from the winery up the road to also participate in the University's program. She would say it was a testimony to his sales skills, but the success was likely owed more to his stubbornness. He possessed an obstinate streak, she had discovered, and an unshakable trust in his own knowledge of his profession. She was easily able to understand why he'd been referred to as a know-it-all, because he would argue a point to the death, if it involved one of his bats or butterflies, particularly if he thought he was right, which he usually did.

"I'm very glad that you came to have lunch with me. Otherwise I would've never seen how brown you look in the daytime! What's up with that? Anyway, that guy that was with the kids? He's the one about to be elected mayor."

"I saw your sign," he mumbled. "And it's the dispersion of light particulates. Now I have to worry about what werewolves think?"

"You should be concerned with what *that* werewolf thinks. And more importantly, don't you want to fit in with your friends and neighbors? What are they gonna say about you at your retirement party when your ruff is all old and gray? 'He was a good scientist, but we wish he would have put some pants on?' Think of your legacy."

"I don't have any friends or neighbors," he'd interjected with a grin, showing her a glint of his fangs when she scowled in return.

"Oh, you do too. You said you like the people in your lab! Making friends as an adult is hard, work friends are a good enough start. And if you decide to stay at the university, they'll be your friends and colleagues for years. What'll wind up on your tombstone if you don't put pants on all that time? 'Horny for humans, hater of pants. Oh yeah, something about hummingbirds, we think.'" He'd chirped in agreement, and she laughed again. "Besides, what if I want to take you home someday? What if we want to go on a trip to a place that's not as mixed species as this? I don't want some random floozy sticking her fingers in your cock pocket. Best to cover it up."

She blushed the instant the words were out. The notion of bringing him home to meet her family implied a level of permanence she knew their relationship did not have, but rather than point that out to her, he'd given a nervous click at the thought.

"I'll definitely wear pants for that."

A lifetime of flying being his main mode of transportation meant every inch of him was solid and sinewy, and a lifetime of launching himself from the ground into the sky meant his thighs were thick with muscle and he had an impeccable ass. His wings covered most of his lower half when he was on the ground, and she had learned that the fine velvet covering his body kept him clean; the constantly shedding dust eliminating any ickiness he might've picked up.

He'd assured her with a snort that his *cock pocket* — the words repeated as derisively as he could manage, giving her his most venomous glare — was safe. It practically had a vacuum seal, he'd explained, preventing any contaminants or floozy fingers from getting in if he wasn't already partially aroused. She'd squinted, testing the theory the moment they were inside a changing room at the first shop she pulled him into. Sure enough, the fingertips she normally slipped into him easily met a firm resistance, and she was mollified that he was safe from molestation.

"Yeah well, you still need pants."

The floral archway was late. She was accustomed to the tardiness of vendors, pushing it from mind until the bride and her mother arrived on site, but the absence of the archway of camellias had felt like a dangerous premonition as the white towncar swung onto the drive. Grace could tell immediately that the young woman had been crying.

"Is-is there any way to have more tables added?" she'd asked with a slight hitch in her voice.

Grace frowned. "I suppose we could squeeze them in," she began cautiously, "but it's going to crowd your dance floor. And just because we can set up tables doesn't mean you'll be able to accommodate more than twenty extra people at this point, remember? We went over that with the caterer. There's a wiggle room for another twenty plates, just in case your existing guests bring plus ones they didn't disclose, but those bodies are already accounted for in the existing seating chart."

The bride's mother huffed, the foxtails behind her spreading like a luxurious fan. "See? It can't be done!" She was technically correct, but Grace could tell at that moment her sharp words weren't helping anyone, least of all her daughter.

She cleared her throat, continuing. "If you want to add tables, I'm just the venue manager, I'll do whatever you want. But if you're making room for another fifty or sixty guests, you won't be able to feed them. You don't have favors made up for extra tables, and you don't have floral arrangements. So if I were your planner, I would be cautioning you against it."

The bride's mother threw up her hands, and Grace had a feeling things hadn't actually been settled with the in-laws to be. The kitsune nodded, looking positively wretched, on a day when she should have been glowing with happiness.

"We can make it work," she went on, because stars knew she had pulled a rabbit out of a hat on more than one wedding in the past, magicking up the undoable. "We can pull apart your floral arrangements and make small bouquets for each table, I can instruct the caterer to quarter her cake slices. The servers can decrease the amount of food everyone gets to stretch it. We'll do it if we have to, we can make the best of it. I can call one of the local food trucks, they all do events, so when people are still hungry, which they will be, you can have another round of food that arrives later. That's over your budget, but your budget was made to the guestlist, so it's a consideration." She threw the older kitsune a silencing look, uncaring that she was vastly overstepping.

The young woman worried her full lower lip with sharp teeth as she thought.

"We spent a long time picking out the flowers," she said finally. "Ume for faithfulness, tsubaki for pure love. Carrying a bouquet is a Western tradition, so we're already doing things our own way. I-I don't want to pull apart the arrangements."

Grace sighed, watching the young woman swallow with difficulty.

"Can I give you some advice?" The words had tumbled out of her mouth before she could bite them back, and her cheeks flushed pink the instant they were hanging in the air between her and the tear-streaked kitsune. "You need to talk to your fiancé. Not just about this, but, you know, you just need to be able to *talk* to him. When you're unhappy in two years because you've been bottling everything up since this day, it's all going to come rushing out and it's a lot harder to fix things when you've let them break beyond repair. Just . . . call him right now and let him know that he needs to tell his mother *no*. This is the guest list you wanted, end of story. If they have people that weren't invited today, you could have another small get together for them in a few weeks, give us a call, we're happy to host it again for you. I always offer returning customer discounts. But today isn't about people who there's no room for, it's not about your mother-in-law feeling slighted because she couldn't invite her entire town, and it's not about *your* mother telling you that you need to stand up for yourself." The older woman sniffed, but Grace plowed on, undeterred, wishing she'd given the same advice to countless brides over the years, wishing that someone would have given *her* the advice all those years ago.

"It's about you and your fiancé and the choices you're making for the rest of your life. You're choosing to be together, but *staying* together is hard work. No one tells you that, they make you think that love has to be enough. It's *work*. You have to talk to each other, you have to fix things before they break. And that takes maintenance. Talking is maintenance. So go talk to him."

As soon as the words were out, she realized what a hypocrite she was.

She'd spent half a decade of her life mostly miserable, unable to articulate how broken her relationship was, unsure of how to fix it, unable to ask for help. She spent all her time creating the illusion of happily ever afters for other people, while ignoring the shambles of her own relationship. She'd spent the last several months falling irrevocably in love with this sweet, preciously awkward man, and she hadn't told him how she felt. She hadn't even expressed that she wanted him to stay. *How can you blame him for leaving, when you've not told him the way you feel?*

The next several hours passed in a blur. Her lungs and stomach had braided together, and her heart was knotted somewhere in the middle. It wasn't until the kitsune stood beneath the floral arch with her handsome fiancé, their hands bound together in silk as they spoke the words of their culture, that she realized the gravity of what she had done. Or, she corrected herself, more importantly, what she had *not* done.

She hadn't told him the way she smiled unconsciously every time she thought about his soft little chirps, nor about the way she stroked her arms all afternoon on the morning she woke up with a thin coating of his wing dust on her skin. She hadn't told him how hilarious she found his introverted panic, nor how breathtakingly brave he was for trying to make friends in his crowded lab, for facing crowds with her every weekend, gripping her hand as tightly as he could without causing her injury. She hadn't told him how much she loved burying her face in the thick ruff at his neck, or that being held in his arms as he flew from the farm to his house was the most terrifying thing she'd ever experienced in her entire life and she would be happy to walk everywhere for the rest of her days.

She hadn't told him how sweet his care and consideration was, nor how attractive he was when he spoke about his work. She'd never let on that she'd wanted him to stay, that she wanted to see where their relationship might go if it had room to breathe and grow; wanted to see how deeply she could fall in love with him. She hadn't been looking for love, but something special had, in fact, dropped out of the sky. *And you're going to let him just fly away without a fight.*

"No, I'm not," she whispered. "I'm not."

Caleia had squeaked out a halfhearted protest when Grace plunked the headset on her shiny, sable hair. The cocktail hour was already underway, and the caterers had already set up the dinner service. The photographer was busy with the bridal party, the cake was placed, the flowers were fragrant, and there was nothing left for her to manage.

"I-I have something I need to do. I have something I need to say to someone, and I need to go right now."

Caleia threw up her hands. "Can you at least come back? I don't know what the hell I'm doing!"

"Oh, you do too. You just like playing dumb. Just be bossy, that's what you're good at! If someone needs something, figure out a way to get it for them, it's as simple as that. I'll definitely be back."

The sight of the dark forest looming ahead of her once she'd pulled past the dark barn and run across the unlit field made her heart hammer in her throat. *It's only a little ways in. It's only a little ways in. You know what trees is his, just don't stop until you get there.*

She realized the folly of her plan when she arrived at the base of Merrick's tree unmolested, looking up, and up, and up. She would need to *climb* this staircase, for the first time, the most daunting prospect she'd ever faced. Grace didn't consider herself to be too terribly out of shape — she got her daily steps in at the farm and she wasn't much of a couch potato, the the non-stop spiral of the endless upward climb had her panting by her third circuit of the wide trunk, the buzzing hum of the electrical cables running up the insulated tubing not enough like the sound of his buzzing to motivate her. *You're joining a gym. As soon as the new week starts, your ass is joining a gym.* A glance up showed her how far she still had to climb, and in the end she slumped in defeat. His face appeared over the edge of the balcony when she dialed his mobile number, peering down at her in wonder before he swooped off the railing like a giant bat. *No, not a bat. Like a giant moth.*

"What are you doing here?! I thought today was the wedding!"

She was still panting, wisps of curls pulling from her updo to frame her face, and she didn't need a mirror to know she splotched red and that her hair resembled a poodle.

"It is. It is, but-but I needed to tell you something."

Her mouth ran dry, her jaw working and no sound coming out, Grace wondered if she'd come all this way only to chicken out when it counted. *What is wrong with you!? It's time to leave the Dumb Bitch condominium behind!*

"I-I don't want you to leave. That's what I came to let you know, I *had* to let you know. I don't want you to leave when your program ends. I know there's a job in South America, I know they're probably going to recruit you, but I want you to stay. I know that's selfish, and I know you'll probably say no, but if you left and I hadn't told you, I would regret it forever."

His mouth was hanging open, his antennae plastered to the side of his head, and he gave a small chirp in response, but she pushed on.

"I don't want you to leave. I love spending time with you, and I love the way you laugh and your little chirps and your silly antennae." Tears were running down her face, but she still laughed at the way he huffed at the affront. "I know it's selfish, and I've known from the beginning that you were going to leave, and I shouldn't have fallen in love with you, but I did, and-and I want you to stay. That's-that's it. That's what I came to say."

Merrick threw up his hands in confusion. "What are you *talking* about?! I-I'm going to finish my dissertation here. I decided that about a month ago, I told you about it! Were you *listening*? I've been ABD for so long, and this is such a nice program and it's a really nice school, and the people here . . . the people are actually nice. I want to finish it up here and see if I can get a position. When did I tell you I was leaving?"

"But there was some guy from South America, something about hummingbirds—'

Merrick nodded, gesturing to the empty table behind him. "He was speaking at a conference, and he stopped by to pick up the kiddos. They're ready to go home."

She floundered. She would never trust Tris again. She would never trust gossip and secondhand snark, would never take things Caleia said and form her own shotgun assumptions, and she was going to hang on his every word in the future, no matter how in the weeds he got in discussing his job. He *had* mentioned something about his dissertation, she vaguely remembered, grumbling about not being required to teach if he were postdoc, but she'd been listening with half an ear, too busy looking at . . . too busy looking at the farm's calendar, as she planned the needs for the kitsune's wedding. *Someone else's happily ever after, as usual.* But he was going to stay, and that was all that mattered.

"Say that again." He advanced on her slowly, pulling her into his arms.

"Say-which part, I said a lot of stuff."

His laugh was a low rumble of thunder, a vibration she felt rippling through her.

"The part where you said you fell in love with me."

"It was an accident," she whispered. "I wasn't looking for a relationship. I knew you weren't going to be here long and I-I didn't mean for it to happen. But you're just too damn fluffy to resist."

He smoothed the halo of frizz back off her face, tilting her chin with a velutinous hand.

"That's okay. I fell in love with you very intentionally. That makes up for it, I think."

She was prepared for the kiss, his warm mouth crashing into hers, the nip of his smalfangs tugging at her lips. Nothing she'd been looking for, and somehow everything she'd needed. *He was going to stay.* It was time to create her own happily ever after, Grace thought.

"Go put some gods damned pants on," she whispered against his lips, squealing in laughter when he scooped her up with a squawk of outrage, "so you can come back with me." Here for a good time, and maybe even a long time. "I want to introduce everyone to my boyfriend."

CHAPTER ELEVEN

Moon Blooded Breeding Clinic

JULY 2022

He'd been still chewing over the idea that morning when he saw the flier.

The silhouette of a happy family, a mother cradling an infant to her chest and smiling beatifically beneath the intriguing text which caught his eye.

Are you a healthy werewolf aged 25-40?

We need you! Help families achieve their dreams

-Call us for information today

Lowell read and reread the flier several times, not gleaning any better idea of what service it advertised on the fifth reading than he had on the first, before snapping a photo with his phone.

It was several hours before he got around to calling the number, having finished the arduous task of winterizing the pool with his brother, retreating to the small guesthouse at last to video call his office for a status update, only to be told there was still no change: his travel visa was virtually worthless in the current state of things, he would be stranded stateside for the foreseeable future. *Volunteer work it is*.

He was unprepared for the conversation which resulted.

"What we offer is a revolutionary new way for families to achieve their goal of natural childbirth, particularly those interspecies couples unable to have a child together due to reproductive incompatibility." The doctor to whom his call had been transferred—once he'd answered a brief survey of questions confirming that he was, in fact, a healthy werewolf within the desired age bracket—had an impassioned manner of speaking, and Lowell leaned forward on his elbows, eyebrows drawn as he wondered if this actually constituted as "volunteer" work.

"Our donors are not just contributing genetic material, they are providing the opportunity for these families to end months of frustration and money wasted. Interspecies adoption is cost-prohibitive for most families, as you may know, and the viability of in vitro fertilization is very low for so many people...in contrast, we are not another dead end. Due to the uniqueness of our service, our success rate is unparalleled, I assure you."

Contributing genetic material.

"It's sperm donation," Lowell cut in, attempting to find the straightest path forward, as he always did. "Why do you specifically need werewolves?"

"Ah, that is where you're wrong. The service we provide is far more than merely donating sperm in a specimen cup. The success rate depends on actual copulatory practices, and the unique physiology of the lupine male provides the most effective method to ensure successful insemination."

"On actual..." His cock twitched as he considered the meaning behind the doctor's words. "Actual *intercourse*?" Being trapped in a succession of his brother's homes had been challenging in more ways than one, and he'd not had sex since arriving in Cambric Creek months earlier. Grayson's poolhouse afforded a bit more privacy, but being a Hemming in Cambric Creek was a handicap in and of itself.

"That's correct. You see, a lunar estrus cycle is triggered in each patient..."

The doctor's words fell away as Lowell mentally slotted the final piece of the puzzle together. Lunar estrus was just a fancy term for a heat, and if the copulation would be taking place at the full moon...*the unique physiology of the lupine male.*

"I'd be *knotting* someone?!" His cock twitched again, thickening at the thought. It was an act rarely indulged in; the danger of the turn, the reproductive ramifications, outing oneself as a werewolf—there was much that could go wrong in such a scenario. It was a lecture they'd all received from their father once puberty hit, and from the notes compared with his brother's Jack's speech remained the same from son-to-son: you do *not* knot your partners. The risk of injury was present, the risk of an unwanted pregnancy substantial, and life as a werewolf outside of Cambric Creek's well-sheltered borders was not always a picnic. It was mortifying and he clearly remembered holding his breath, trying to disappear into the cushions of the sofa as his father paced agitatedly before him and Owen, but the lecture had stuck. He'd had more partners than he could count who'd been disappointed he'd *not* knotted them, not understanding that the *unique physiology* was something that came with the turn. *And these people are willing to pay for it!*

On the other end of the line, the doctor cleared his throat.

"We don't like to use that term, but yes, essentially. The breeding instinct triggered by the smell of a receptive female coupled with the reproductive advantage of the bulbus glandis is quite sufficient to—"

The breeding instinct. Completely animalistic, mindless rutting, over and over into a woman in heat who would be writhing and begging for his cock, for his knot; tightening around him as he filled her repeatedly, again and again until he was spent and she was full of his seed. Lowell shifted, his erection practically scraping the table's underside. *It's been a very long summer...*

"The process is completely safe. Everything happens in our clinic, and the safety of both the donor and recipient is our utmost concern. If you are worried about being unduly othered, let me put your fears to rest—the clinic founders and all its doctors are of the lupine persuasion, and we take the privacy of our donors very seriously. You will be in good hands with us."

Lowell thought about Jackson's little boy again, the over-whelming joy of watching him learn new things and explore the world...he could give that gift to another family. He was a Hemming, a highly sought-after bloodline, and he had no plans to tie himself down to a mortgage and family in Cambric Creek, not anytime soon, despite his mother's wishes. The donor werewolves were compensated, and he could donate those funds back to the clinic, or to another charity.

The clinic itself was in Starling Heights, a decent enough distance from Cambric Creek to ensure he'd not likely run into anyone who would know him. Devotion to family, loyalty to pack, service to community, that's what his parents were always going on about. There seemed no better service to the community than to help a family achieve their desire for a child...and the fact that he would actually get to enjoy the process was all the better.

"I'll do it," he blurted, knuckles tightening on the table. He was going stir crazy, the open road normally before him abruptly curtailed, and he needed something to break up the monotony of his new non-routine. He could help a family, could do something worthwhile with his time for as long as he was stuck here. And it won't be so terrible for you either, he thought, an end to the hometown dry spell. "Where do I sign?"

Pre-Order Now: https://amzn.to/3wVOr3B

CHAPTER TWELVE

Wolves & Warriors

JUNE 2022

Get bitten, abducted, dominated, and claimed by these SMOKING HOT alpha-hole baddies...

Whether you prefer your hero dark and brooding, sweet and sensual, monstrous or beautiful, we've got him ready and waiting to give you exactly what you desire.

This collection holds nothing back with all the tension that drives you wild and all the panty-melting steam you crave. Rouse your desire for top-notch paranormal romance with 16 all new books, and then keep reading for 5 equally enticing stories of the sci fi variety.

Shifters, vampires, demons, and more are ready and waiting to bend you over that bed and pound their stories into your brain until you're panting, moaning, and screaming for more.

Think you can stand the heat? **https://amzn.to/3sRXZuI**

About Author

C.M. Nascosta is an author and professional procrastinator from Cleveland, Ohio. As a child, she thought that living on Lake Erie meant one was eerie by nature, and her corresponding love of all things strange and unusual started young. She's always preferred beasts to boys, the macabre to the milquetoast, the unknown darkness in the shadows to the Chad next door. She lives in a crumbling old Victorian with a scaredy-cat dachshund, where she writes nontraditional romances featuring beastly boys with equal parts heart and heat, and is waiting for the Hallmark Channel to get with the program and start a paranormal lovers series.

Do you love exclusive short stories and character art? Consider supporting me on Patreon!

https://www.patreon.com/Monster_Bait

Follow

Visit C.M. Nascosta's website for Content Warnings, blog
posts, and newsletter signup: cmnascosta.com
Stay in touch on social media!
facebook.com/authorcmnascosta
twitter.com/cmnascosta
instagram.com/cmnascosta

A weekend with friends, fun in the sun, and huge, naked
orcs. What could be better? That's what three suburban elves
think when they book a trip to an orc nudist resort, well
known for its libidinous residents and hedonistic parties. Ris,
Lurielle, and Silva arrive with plans to sample the DTF locals
and work on their tans, *not* catch feelings. When Lurielle

meets a syrupy-voiced gentleman who seems interested in more than just a weekend fling, she finds sticking to the plan is easier said than done. From a public bathhouse to a back alley pub, the trip has unintended consequences on the lives of the three work friends and the orcs they meet. Can a weekend of no-strings sex actually end in love?

Made in United States
North Haven, CT
20 October 2022